EDDY JOHNSON,
BOOK DEALER

Book Design & Production:
Columbus Publishing Lab
www.ColumbusPublishingLab.com

Paperback ISBN: 978-1-63337-569-7
E-Book ISBN: 978-1-63337-570-3

Printed in the United States of America
1 3 5 7 9 10 8 6 4 2

EDDY JOHNSON,
BOOK DEALER

John Wiley

Boyle
&
Dalton

For Marie and Boots

AUSTIN, TEXAS

1987

The global recession of 1980-82 created a wave of immigration into Texas from places like Brooklyn and New Jersey, Chicago, Philadelphia, and Boston. These immigrants came in search of a fresh start. But they brought a lot of baggage with them too—personal stuff, as well as deeply ingrained cultural traditions. They changed Texas forever...

CHAPTER I

TUESDAY AFTERNOON around four-thirty I'm over on North Lamar, visiting with Johnny Paoli in the back room of his bookstore.

I don't go see Johnny much. Usually when I do it's a waste of time. He's greedy. When he's making a deal, he needs to know he's the only guy coming out ahead. It's frustrating because he has a lot of important books. He's been collecting for decades and, at the prices he asks, he's sold almost nothing. His stockpile is enormous.

The book I've come to see him about is a first edition of *Mardi* by Herman Melville. I got a request for it in my P.O. box last week from a lady in Maryland, and Johnny's the only guy in town who's got one. It's been gathering dust in his store for six years. He's got it marked at eight-fifty, two hundred above what it looks up at in mint condition. And Johnny's copy is not mint. It's slightly molded for one thing. And the opening endpaper of the first volume is defaced by an inscription dated 1850: *To Joshua Cooper, on the occasion of his 18th birthday, from his brother Samuel Cooper.*

Johnny's sitting across from me behind his desk, going on and on about his problems. Business is bad. It's a miracle he manages to keep from going under. He's getting squeezed from every direction and now, on top of everything, he's having trouble with his back. An operation he might need is way beyond his means.

I tell him, "Hey. Maybe you should have a sale. Clear out some of that stuff that's been hanging around too long."

"A sale?" Johnny says. "No, I don't think so."

"There's nothing to it. It would be over before you know it."

"Sure. In the blink of an eye. And when the dust settles, all my best books would be gone. My catalogue destroyed."

"I don't know. You might try it. You could advertise it in the paper. *Paoli Books' Big Blowout Sale! Everything Half Price All Weekend!*"

"Stop it. Jesus. I can't reduce my prices."

"Come on, Johnny. There's stuff you've been holding onto forever. You got troubles? I'm telling you—as a friend—you need to learn to bend a little."

"Sure. Bend over. That's what you're saying."

"Aw, Johnny, I don't know why I bother."

"You've got a buyer for one of my books."

"No, I'm just saying, in general, you need to loosen up a little."

"What book?" Johnny says. He's all excited. "Is it the Steinbeck?"

"The Melville."

"The Melville! How much will they pay?"

"I'll give you five hundred."

"*You*," Johnny says. "*You'll* give me."

"That's right. I give you five hundred, I pass the book along, I make forty, maybe fifty bucks. Just enough to make it worth my while."

"Yeah, right."

"Jeez, Johnny, what do you think? You got it marked two hundred over the price guides."

"Screw the price guides."

"Okay, fine." I stand. "Just forget I mentioned it." I walk to the door. "I'll tell you something, Johnny. You wonder why your store's not doing better. Maybe it's because everyone in Austin knows how cheap you are."

"That's not true," he says. "What do I have to do to satisfy you dealers? Go bankrupt?"

I grab the doorknob.

"Eddy, wait a minute."

I look back at him.

He says, "About the Melville."

"Yeah?"

"Well, since you got no use for it, maybe you could give *me* the buyer," he says.

"Are you serious?"

"What would you be losing?" he asks.

"I'll tell you what. I'll give you the buyer for twenty bucks."

"You'd sell it to me?"

"Sure. Information leading to an eight-hundred-dollar transaction? You bet."

"They'll go eight hundred?"

"Depending on how much they mind the inscription."

I pull the lady's letter from the breast pocket of my jacket and hold it up so Johnny can see it.

"Twenty bucks," I say.

"Five dollars."

"Fifteen," I say.

"Five dollars, Eddy." He gets his wallet out, grabs a five, and hands it to me. I give him the letter.

CHAPTER 2

I'M DRIVING SOUTH ON LAMAR—heading back to my room—when I notice the Sisters of Mercy Thrift Shop and decide to check it out. It's been a week.

I park my truck in front and get out. I hear a guy's voice saying, "Eddy. Hey, Eddy." It's Jimmy Waller, a book dealer I know. He's coming toward me on the sidewalk.

I like Jimmy. We've never done any deals—he specializes in heraldry and military history, and all I ever handle is modern literature. But we get along.

I'm glad to see Jimmy. Could be he owes me a favor. A couple months back I gave his number to a retired colonel I met who'd lost an arm at Diem Phu. Since retiring, he'd become an avid collector of books about Vietnamese history and culture, Asian cuisine, and helicopters. I got the impression he was ready to pay top dollar. Maybe he'd given Jimmy a call, done some business.

Jimmy walks up to me on the sidewalk. We're both smiling. We shake hands.

"How's it going, Eddy? Long time no see."

"I'm doing okay."

"Glad to hear it."

"How about you?"

"Pretty good," he says. "You know."

"Tell me something. Did a guy ever call you? Guy with one arm? Wanted stuff about Vietnam?"

Jimmy says, "You gave that guy my number?"

I nod.

"He spent six hundred bucks with me. Thanks, man."

"No problem."

"Hey, you going to the book show?"

"I guess so. I was gonna check around, see if anybody wants to split a table. Not many people come looking for literature. You military guys always seem to make out."

"You got that right."

"What do you sell, mostly? Civil War stuff?"

"Yeah. And anything with a swastika on the cover. You know. I don't do as well as Texana dealers, though."

"Texana!" I say. "Don't even get me started on Texana! I saw Tommy Grummel last week. He was over at Billy Joe Anderson's store. He was selling some old maps and stuff. He told me he'd just sold a Texana book that morning for three grand. Guess what the title was."

"What?"

"*Cow Poop along the Brazos.*"

Jimmy laughs.

"It drives me nuts," I say. "I spend all my time messing around with, like, Nobel Prize winners, and I can hardly make ends meet."

"It's over my head," Jimmy says.

"Hey listen, Jimmy. What are you doing Friday? A bunch of the guys are gonna be at the Dusty Jacket. It's Ken Wright's birthday."

"Wish I could, Eddy. My wife's got friends coming over. I'll probably end up playing Trivial Pursuit all night."

"Wait a minute. You're married?" I say.

"Almost a year now. You didn't know?"

"I never heard you got married. Congratulations. I mean…I guess it's still working out and everything…"

Jimmy laughs. "Maybe you should try it, Eddy."

"I don't think so."

"Well, I got to go," he says. "I'm glad I ran into you. You goin' in the thrift shop?"

"Yeah, I thought I'd take a quick look."

"Good luck," he says. "I hope you find something."

"Thanks. And don't forget you owe me. I know that guy with one arm didn't haggle worth a damn."

"I'll try to remember. You be sure and keep reminding me, though. See you at the show, Eddy."

"See ya."

CHAPTER 3

I GO IN THE THRIFT SHOP. It's one big room crammed with racks of old clothes. Clothes are mostly what they sell. Along the walls—on shelves—there are old garden tools and suitcases, punch bowls and ice cream makers and black-and-white TVs. The books are whatever happens to be in cardboard boxes on the floor in the back by the dressing rooms.

"Good afternoon, sister," I say to the nun behind the counter. Sister Francine, I think her name is.

"Mr. Johnson," she says. "We just got some books in. Three boxes."

"Hey, that's terrific. Must be my lucky day."

"The Lord does love to give."

Yeah right, I think. I walk to the back where the books are.

I spot the three boxes right away, all of them big and full of hardbacks. I get on my knees and start going through them. The first box is all book club fiction. Lots of mysteries, science fiction. I move on to the second box and dig about halfway down through pretty much the same kind of stuff. And then I find it. It's bigger than the others. A publisher's edition—an old one—of George Orwell's *1984*. It's in nice shape. The dust jacket is primo. I open it up and look at its publishing history and see it's a first edition. It's an American first, but still, I can get thirty bucks for it.

I put it down next to me and dig through the rest of the books. I don't find anything else. I pick up the Orwell, get to my feet, and head to the counter. I am one satisfied customer. The great thing about finding a book at the Sisters of Mercy Thrift Shop is that the nuns who run the place don't know anything about books—I guess they just read the Bible—and so they charge a flat rate of twenty-five cents, no matter what book it is.

The nun sees me coming. She sees the book in my hand and says, "You found a good one, Mr. Johnson?"

"A pretty good one, Sister."

I pull a quarter from my pants pocket and hand it to her. She puts the money away and writes me a receipt.

"It's so sweet of you," she says, "taking the time to shop for your poor mother."

"It's the least I can do, Sister."

"Such a good son. I hope she's doing better."

CHAPTER 4

BACK IN MY ROOM at the Alamo Boardinghouse, I'm sitting on the bed with the phone in my lap. I dial Bill Holland's number. There are some rings, then a guy says, "Bernie's Bookshelves."

"This is a friend of Bill's," I say.

The guy says, "How's the weather?"

"Lousy. It's been raining so much there are puddles you could swim in."

The guy doesn't say anything.

"Laps," I say. "Puddles you could swim laps in."

"Hold on," he says. There's a click and Bill comes on the line.

"Yeah?" Bill says.

"Bill, it's Eddy."

"Hey, Eddy. You feeling lucky? What'll it be?"

"What's the Vegas line on James Michener's *Rhode Island*?" A novel that made the bestseller list the minute it was published. In thirteen weeks, it's climbed to number five. I've got a feeling it could go as high as three this week. Last night—one shopping day before the list is compiled—Michener appeared on Johnny

Carson and looked good. Got the audience laughing, got a big hand when he left. Hell, his book could jump to number two. I've seen it happen plenty of times.

"Vegas don't like it," Bill says. "Three-to-two it stays where it is. You want up?"

"To number three."

"Five-to-two."

"Okay. One hundred dollars on *Rhode Island* to number three."

"You and everybody else."

"Hey, Michener's a superstar. His first printings are huge— like a million or something."

"The guy's old news, Eddy. He's over the hill. Besides, who cares about Rhode Island?"

"Vegas is gonna eat this one," I say.

"Anything else?"

"Yeah. Thirty on the L'Amour to drop to seventeen." It's been on the list 168 weeks.

"Okay, thirty to seventeen," Bill says. "You got it."

"Thanks, Bill."

I hang up the phone. I go in the bathroom and get the bottle of bourbon that's in the medicine cabinet. I pour some bourbon in the glass I have, carry the glass into my room, and sit in the chair by the window. I'm on the third floor. Looking down, I can see my truck parked across the street.

The phone rings and I answer it.

"Mr. Johnson?" a guy's voice says.

"That's me."

"I don't know if you remember me. I'm Don Mulligan. I met

you about a year ago. I run a self-storage facility out in Round Rock. Liberty Store-N-Go."

I can't place him.

"You told me if I ever had books to sell, you might come look at them."

"Sure," I say. "Why? What you got?"

"I had a customer abandon a unit this week. I cut the padlock and went in. There's a bunch of stuff—furniture, mostly—but also some books."

I listen while he tries to describe them. I can't tell from what he's saying whether they're hardback or paperback, what shape they're in, or whether there's a hundred books or a thousand.

I interrogate him a little and decide to go see them.

"I could swing by later this week. Maybe Friday. Does that work?"

"Sure. I'm here every day till four."

I get a pen and paper. I tell him I'm ready, and he gives me the address and his phone number. It's probably nothing, but longshots are my bread and butter.

I finish the bourbon and put my jacket on. I start to grab my truck keys but decide instead to walk to Joe Bob's Grille.

CHAPTER 5

GOOD OLD JOE BOB'S.

Austin's got plenty of cheap dive restaurants. The trouble is they all get discovered. Yuppies descend like locusts. Pretty soon there's a *New York Times* machine by the front door and BMWs and Volvos circling the block. It takes an hour to get a table.

I've lost almost all the good old spots that way. But not Joe Bob's Grille. With its filthy toilet, its yellowed Dr. Pepper clock-and-menu, its squeeze jars of margarine on every table—it's my oasis in a city turning cute and expensive.

At seven o'clock, I'm the only customer in the place. I'm in my usual booth, my back against the greasy wall, digesting. The waitress—a biker mamma with a skull-and-bones tattoo on her arm—is in the kitchen or out in the alley blowing a joint. I haven't seen her since she dropped off my chicken fried steak.

I'm facing the street, so I notice when a little red roadster swings out of traffic and parks in front of Joe Bob's. A young woman gets out of the car. She's gorgeous, all dolled up and wearing heels.

When she's steady on her feet, she heads for the entrance to Joe Bob's, pulls the door open, and comes in. She walks a few steps into the room, then stops. It occurs to me I could be hallucinating.

I'm watching her, taking in her face, when she looks over and sees me.

I smile a little.

"Excuse me," she says. "Are you Edward Johnson?"

"I am," I say, amazed.

She comes over to my booth.

I say, "How'd you get my name?"

"It was given to me by a friend. He told me you are a person whose business it is to locate and identify rare books."

"How'd you find me?"

"Someone at your boardinghouse said you'd be here. Mr. Johnson, I need your help."

"You can sit if you want to," I say.

"Thank you." She sits across from me.

"A friend of yours recommended me?"

"He told me that people in your profession are not altogether honest, but that you are something of a gentleman. Someone who can be trusted."

"Well, I was raised by decent people."

"Then may I take you into my confidence?"

"Sure," I say. "I don't mind. You can start by telling me your name."

"I'm Peggy Miller."

"Peggy Miller," I say. "Isn't your father—"

"Frank Miller," she says.

Big Frank Miller. Candidate for mayor. His face is plastered all over the city—on billboards and buses, in full-page newspaper ads. He's leading his opponent—the incumbent Travis—by double digits. The election is one month away.

"Your father's going to be the next mayor of Austin."

"Yes, I suppose."

"You don't seem all that excited."

"Oh, I want Daddy to win. It's just such an inconvenience dealing with the public. Everything's so sensitive. Really, that's the reason I'm here, Mr. Johnson. When Daddy decided to become mayor, we had to get rid of some servants. Apparently, it's wrong to have so many, so we had to let some go. One of them, a woman named Maria Juarez who worked in the pantry, took some things when she left, last Friday.

"She must have overheard Daddy sometime or other bragging about this particular book he has. It's like a hundred and fifty years old and autographed. Daddy has a big library, lots of first editions and manuscripts and things."

"I've never done any business with him."

"I wouldn't think so. The thing is, this book is one of the most valuable in Daddy's collection. He had it appraised at twenty thousand dollars. And this Maria, this pantry assistant, took it."

"And other things?"

"Nothing much. Some cans of food, we think. Her uniform shoes."

"How do you know she took it?"

"This. It was in our mailbox this morning." She opens her purse, gets out a folded piece of paper, and hands it to me. I open it up and look it over. It's written in pencil, crude and heavy: *We* *have the book that was under glass. $500 if you want it back. Maria will call. No police.*

It's signed *Raoul.*

"I want you to buy the book from her," Peggy Miller says. "I've just got to get it back. Daddy doesn't know it's missing. He has a replica of the original and I put that in the display case. Now I've got to get the real one back before he notices."

"Has Maria called?"

"Yes. This afternoon. We agreed to do the transaction tonight at ten, at a discreet location I've arranged. In the warehouse of a friend of my father's."

"In three hours," I say.

She nods.

"I don't know…"

"You've just got to help me, Mr. Johnson. That book means so much to Daddy, and I'm in charge of the servants, so it's all my fault… If I don't get that book back, I don't know what I'll do."

"What book is it?" I say.

She pulls an index card from her purse and slides it across the table. I read aloud the info typed on it: "*Dear Sweet Texas,* by Herman Arnold; 1826; first edition; mint; autographed."

It's an incredibly rare book—much rarer than anything I've ever handled. Only two hundred copies were printed. Arnold wrote that one book, then he was killed at the Alamo.

"Daddy's little Arnold. Do you know it?" she asks.

"I've heard of it, but I've never 'seen one. I'm not a Texana dealer. I'd have to research it some before I could be sure of identifying it correctly."

"My friend suggested I give you this." She pulls a small, thick

pamphlet from her purse and hands it to me. It's a 17th edition
McBride's Guide to Texas Titles.

"Look," I say, putting the pamphlet down. "I'm sorry for
your trouble. I just don't think I'm the right—"

"I am prepared to offer you two hundred dollars."

"Four hundred."

"I can only offer two."

"There's no knowing who will show up at that warehouse.
Maybe Raoul, who's bound to be better with a knife or a gun
than he is with a pencil. Four hundred is the very least my neck
is worth."

"My friend warned me you would—"

"Maybe your friend should get the book for you."

She doesn't say anything.

"There's danger in this job," I say. "I can smell it. And I don't
like that I'm stumbling into it at the last minute, with nothing but
what you say to clue me in. I don't even know you."

"Everything I have told you is the truth."

"Three hundred."

"How about this?" she says. "I'll give you one hundred dollars now, as a retainer. If you get the book, I will pay you another
two hundred. When I get the book."

I think about it. I figure this is probably as good as I'm going
to do with someone who counts cans of food in their pantry.

"Okay," I say. "It's a deal."

We don't shake hands.

She says, "Naturally, considering the value of the book, I
will want my chauffeur to accompany you. He'll pick you up and
take you to the warehouse. He'll bring the five hundred dollars for

Maria. When you have completed the transaction, he will pay you your two hundred and return you to your residence."

"Okay."

She pulls a crisp, new hundred from her purse and hands it to me. I put it away.

"Now I really must be going," she says. She stands, gets stable on her heels, and makes for the door with lots of little steps.

She turns and faces me before going out.

"Charles will be at your boardinghouse at nine-thirty. Please be ready."

Then she's gone—back inside her cute little car and speeding away.

I leave too. I grab a toothpick for the walk back to my room.

CHAPTER 6

AT EIGHT-THIRTY, it's dark outside the window. I'm in the armchair, some more bourbon in my glass, reading what the *McBride's* says about *Dear Sweet Texas*.

It's considered the first Texas epic poem. It's autobiographical: the story of a convicted bank robber who escapes from a Georgia prison, digs up some buried loot, and flees to Texas. He buys a ranch in the Brazos Valley, gets a herd and a wife, and settles down. A lot of the poem revolves around his struggles with the land and the unpredictability of cattle prices.

McBride's says that the poem, "…though sentimental and in many ways crude…owing to Arnold's illiteracy (the poem was dictated, over a five-year period, to his wife)…is nevertheless appealing and relevant to modern Texas readers, largely by virtue of its digressions from the personal story of the reformed robber to ode-like outbursts of praise for Texas…"

Quotes from the poem are included as examples:

Dear sweet Texas how I love you.
Grass so green, sky so blue.
Where a man can do the things a man has got to do. (1)

Texas you've been good to me.
I'm as happy and free as a squirrel in a tree.
I'll someday be buried under thee. (132)

There's more of the same—the kind of stuff Texana lovers go crazy over—but I can't stomach it. I flip ahead to means of identification. There's one sure thing listed: page 68, six lines from the bottom; an overlooked typo corrected in posthumous printings: the word *bluebonnets* appearing as *blusbonnets*.

I put the pamphlet down. I go to the closet, get my shoulder holster, and put it on. Then I go to the desk and get my pistol from the drawer. It's already loaded. I put it in the holster, snug against me, and put my jacket on.

I'm not taking any chances on this job. I wasn't born and raised in Pflugerville. People as rich as the Millers don't give money away. If Peggy Miller is willing to pay three hundred dollars for a couple hours' work, there must be a catch.

Walking to my room from Joe Bob's, I was thinking of a book dealer I used to know. Russ Martin, from Cincinnati. He got knocked off two years ago during what must have seemed like a routine job. A buyer from out of town called and said he wanted a first edition Thomas Wolfe Russ had listed in the ABA. Could Russ bring it by the Sahara Motel, room 216? Russ drove over with the Wolfe and went in the motel room unarmed and off his guard. And the buyer—once he'd made sure the book was a true first, I guess—pulled a pistol and shot Russ four times. Russ was good, one of the best, but he'd screwed up that one time, in a business that doesn't allow a man mistakes. I didn't go to the funeral.

CHAPTER 7

I'M SITTING ON THE STOOP of the Alamo in the warm night air. It's almost nine-thirty. Peggy Miller said she was sending her chauffeur. Does that mean I'm waiting for a limo? On the stoop with me is a guy from the second floor I don't know who doesn't like smoking in his room. When one Marlboro gets down to the filter, he uses it to light the next one before flicking it to the curb.

His name is Sam. He never stops talking, and I don't much mind. He drives a bus for the city. He moved to Austin from Chicago six months ago after his wife left him. He tells me, "I'm saving up to get an apartment. I'd like to find a place where I can have a pet. A dog or a cat—something to keep me company."

"I don't like cats," I say, playing along like it's a conversation.

"Anyway, we're all going to have to move. They're going to tear this place down."

"They been saying that since I moved in five years ago," I say. "Don't worry."

"No, man, I seen it on the news. Some dude bought up the whole block. *The fall of the Alamo.* They said it used to be a hotel."

A dark green Ford Taurus pulls to the curb in front of us. The driver gets out. He's a young guy, fit and relaxed, wearing khakis and a plaid button-down shirt. He comes around the Taurus and says, "Are either of you gentlemen Eddy Johnson?"

"Charles?" I say.

He nods.

"Well, this is my ride," I tell Sam.

Charles opens the rear curbside door of the Taurus and holds it for me. He must be used to having passengers ride in back.

I get in and he shuts the door. In the shadows next to me is a plastic baby seat (empty, thank God) and what looks like a diaper bag. Charles goes around and gets behind the wheel.

"Sorry about the car," he says. "It's my wife's. Mine is in the shop."

I pull a little stuffed parrot out from behind my butt and toss it into the baby seat.

"They make you use your own car?" I say.

"I get mileage. Miss Miller didn't want me to use the limo for this. Trying to keep a low profile."

"I understand. I'm part of that low profile."

He laughs. "Yeah, I guess you are."

He pulls into traffic and we head east, then turn left and start up Congress Avenue—the after-hours stillness of it: darkened lunchrooms and menswear shops and the lobbies of big new office towers. Ahead of us, bathed in exterior lighting, is the dome of the capitol building.

At 11th Street we turn east.

Charles says, "Your boardinghouse was on the news. They're going to tear it down."

"So they say."

"I didn't think people still lived there."

We cross over I-35 on the 11th Street bridge.

"Where we headed?" I say.

"Way out on East 12th Street."

"How long have you worked for the Millers?"

"A couple years."

"How are they?"

"They're okay."

"And Maria Juarez?"

"What about her?"

"Do you know her?"

"Not really. She seemed nice enough."

"So, not a hardcore type?"

"Not at all. She's a single mom, a little serious. She seemed tired a lot. If she stole stuff, she must have been desperate. The Millers didn't give any severance, they just told folks not to come back the next day. It was pretty rough."

Eastbound—the interstate well behind us—we pass dingy little bars and used tire shops, funky motels that rent by the week. I settle back and watch Austin's eastside go by: a shabby testament to the meanness of segregation.

CHAPTER 8

THE WAREHOUSE IS at 10035 East 12th, all by itself, way out where there's hardly anything left of the city. It's a big, unmarked building. Charles turns into its gravel parking lot, pulls to within fifty yards of the warehouse, and stops. He kills the engine and turns the lights off.

"So, how do we do this?" I say.

"I'm to stay in the car. When you complete the transaction, I drive you home."

"And what if I don't come back?"

"I leave without you."

"What the hell?" I say.

"I was thinking I'd wait twenty minutes. Is that enough time?"

"I don't know. I guess so."

"Sorry. That's how Miss Miller wants it."

"Okay, but look. If you leave without me, get to a pay phone and call the police. Ask for a detective named Jernigan." Jernigan's a cop I sometimes feed tips to. He's hardly a friend, but he's in my debt a little. "If Jernigan's not available—"

"But Miss Miller was adamant there could be no police."

"So, basically, if anything goes wrong, I'm screwed?"

"I believe you will be needing this." Charles reaches a letter-sized envelope to me. I take the envelope, open it, and count the money. It's the five hundred for Maria. Ten fifties. I put them in my jacket pocket.

I look at my watch. It's 10:05. "Twenty minutes," I say. I get out of the car.

There's nothing but darkness and the sound of crickets.

The warehouse has been empty a long time. Some windows high up, dozens of little panes, are mostly broken. The main entrance—a garage door you could back a semi into—is padlocked and rusted, covered with graffiti. Farther along the wall there are two windows and a metal man door with a hole where its handle used to be. I push the door in slowly, keeping to one side, my other hand on the butt of my holstered gun.

"Hello?" I say.

There's no answer.

"Hello?" I call. "Maria? Peggy Miller sent me. I've got your money."

Still no answer.

I pull my gun out, hold it up, and step through the doorway, into a little office. There's a desk and some filing cabinets shrouded with dust and cobwebs. It's dark, but there's enough moonlight coming in the windows that I can make it all out, including a wooden coat rack next to another door, one that must lead to the warehouse itself.

I get to the side of that door, reach across, and push it in.

"Maria?" I shout. "Maria Juarez…"

My voice echoes through what sounds like a cavernous space.

I step through the second doorway. It's totally dark, I can't see a thing. I crouch against the wall and listen. It must be a huge room. Far off, water is dripping slowly, each drop, as it hits, reverberating.

"I've got your money…"

I listen some more, then get my penlight out. I hold it away from me, up and to my right, and turn it on.

A gun barks. There's a flash a long way off—maybe a hundred feet—and the noise of a bullet hitting the wall above my head. I turn the penlight off.

Keeping low, I move away from where I was, about twenty feet to my left. Away from the little patch of moonlight spilling in through the office door.

Outside, in the parking lot, the Taurus starts up. Then it's moving, crunching gravel as it picks up speed. I hear its tires spin at the edge of the gravel, then it races back toward town. I guess that's another thing Peggy Miller told Charles—to bug out if there's any gun play.

Now it's just me and my gun and the other guy and his. Somehow, I don't think I'm dealing with Maria. Raoul, maybe? I figure I better let him know I'm armed before he gets any ideas. I remember where the flash was the best I can, aim there, and shoot.

There's a yell and the thud of a body falling.

"Aw shit," a man's voice says.

I don't move. I hear him groaning. After a while he gets to his feet. He starts walking away, dragging one leg a little. I let him go. There's a little light when he opens a door at the far end of the warehouse, and for a moment I see his silhouette—tall and narrow—as he staggers outside.

A car starts up. One of its doors slams and it takes off. I run back through the office and outside to see if I can make the car, but it never comes around the warehouse. I hear it going away on the gravel of some other road.

I go in the warehouse and look around with my penlight. I walk all through the big room, seeing what I can as I go, in the pale little orb of light I'm carrying. The place is empty. All I see is bare concrete floor.

Over where the guy was when I shot him, I find some blood, not as much as I expected. There's something else. Small and round—a metal button. I hold it up to my penlight and read it. *Re-Elect Mayor Travis.* It must have come off the guy when he fell. I put it in my pocket.

Before I leave the warehouse, I go through the drawers of the desk in the office. The bottom drawer is full of unopened envelopes addressed to Bart Robinson—the millionaire Texana dealer. There are electric and phone bills, invoices from publishing houses. And letters from the IRS.

Outside, on the road, I start walking back to town. There's no traffic. I figure I'll have to hike two, three miles before I find a pay phone. Then I can call a cab. I should be in town in an hour or two. In plenty of time to drop by Peggy Miller's and refresh her on a few points of etiquette.

CHAPTER 9

THE MILLERS LIVE IN WEST AUSTIN, high above the pettiness of the city—the hustling to get through yellow lights or to a liquor store before it closes or out of the way of ambulances. The streets ascending into West Austin are all dead ends. There's no through traffic, only the quiet comings and goings of the privileged few.

The Miller place has a wall around it. There's a wrought iron gate where the driveway goes in.

It's almost midnight when I pull my truck up to the gate. Outside my window, there's a metal box mounted on a post. It has a button and an oval grate that looks like a speaker.

I roll my window down, reach over, and push the button. I wait, then push it again. I hold it down.

"Yes?" a woman's voice says. It's Peggy Miller.

"Surprise party for Miss Peggy Miller," I say. "All her dearest friends."

"Who is this?" she says.

"Eddy Johnson."

"Mr. Johnson! Do you have the book?"

"Sure. Why not?"

"I'm opening the gate."

There's a buzz and the gate slides open. I drive uphill toward the house on a cobblestone driveway, through the shadows of oak and pecan trees. What a layout. There are trim pebbled paths winding among the flower beds, now and then a flat marble bench where you can sit and contemplate your investments or worry over the difference between the Bahamas and the Riviera. The house itself—as big as a hotel—is classical, Jeffersonian, with tall white columns and uncurtained windows of handmade glass.

I park my truck in front of the house and walk up wide marble steps to the entrance. I bang a brass spaniel's head a couple times, and Peggy Miller opens the door. She's dressed casually now—scotch plaid wraparound, silk blouse, shiny black loafers.

Her eyes are quick and nervous. It's my hands they go to first. She sees I am not holding the book and her eyes jump up—fierce and questioning.

"Where is it?" she says.

"Can I come in?"

"Where's the book?"

"I never even saw it."

"Wasn't Maria at the warehouse?"

"Are you going to let me in or what?"

"Oh darn…darn…" she says, standing aside so I can come in. "It went all wrong…"

She shuts the door behind me.

"Follow me," she says. "We'll talk in the den."

I get ushered through a door opening onto the foyer and find myself in a man's room: walnut paneled, with a pair of leather sofas and a big stone fireplace. There's an oil painting of a race-horse on one wall with a little light trained on it.

Peggy Miller shuts us in and gestures for me to sit on one of the sofas. She sits across from me.

"What happened?" she says.

"Maria never showed."

"Why not? I don't understand."

"How the hell should I know?"

"There's no need to be vulgar."

"Not unless you've just had someone using you for target practice."

"Charles said a shot was fired."

"Shots," I say. "He didn't hang around long enough to hear the rest of them."

"You weren't injured, I hope. You seem all right."

"I'm okay."

"I'm sorry for how things went, but I hope you can understand my need to take precautions."

"Oh, I understand," I say. "Walking back to town, I had plenty of time to figure it out."

"I can't imagine why Maria wasn't there. I'm sure she needs the money."

"All I know is, I wasn't the only one waiting for her at the warehouse. There were some other guys who showed up before Charles and I did."

"Who?"

"I thought maybe you could say."

"I've no earthly idea."

"Yeah? Well, someone gave them the invite, and it wasn't me

and it doesn't make sense that it would be Maria. Who else knew about the meeting? Your friend who recommended me, maybe? The guy who owns the warehouse?"

It's a line of questioning I can tell she doesn't like.

"Think about it," I say.

But she starts feeling sorry for herself instead. "Oh, what does it matter anyway?" she says. "I just know I'm never going to get Daddy's book back now. Why does there have to be such ugliness in the world? Why can't people behave?"

"You might not understand this, but to some folks, twenty grand is a lot of money."

"Sometimes, I wish I were back at Miss Simpson's Academy." Then she says, "I suppose you better give me the five hundred dollars."

"Three hundred," I say.

"What?"

"Call it my cab fare back to town. Unexpected expenses. Really, you should be giving me another two hundred instead of me giving you three."

She arches an eyebrow.

"You still want the book, don't you?" I say.

"Certainly."

"Well, let me try to get it for you. If I get it, you pay me the original two hundred I have coming, plus another two hundred for what happened tonight. If I don't get the book, I'll give you back three hundred."

"I don't know…"

"What else are you going to do? Besides, you and I have already gone to all the trouble of getting to know each other."

Out in the foyer there's the noise of someone opening the front door. There are heavy footsteps—toward the center of the foyer—then a man's voice calling, "Peg?! Peg?! Where are you?!"

CHAPTER 10

PEGGY MILLER SAYS. "Oh God, it's Daddy." She leans forward and whispers, "He mustn't know anything about this. I'll think of a story for you being here. Just follow my lead."

"Peg?!" Miller is trying other doors, opening and shutting them.

"In here, Daddy."

The door opens and in comes her father. Big Frank Miller. The next mayor of Austin if the polls are right. They don't call him Big Frank for nothing. He's well over six feet tall, broad-shouldered and barrel-chested. He's handsome, with some silver in his hair and a good tan. He's wearing cowboy boots.

"What in the hell?" he says, seeing me—a guy in the den with his daughter this late at night.

"Daddy," Peggy Miller says, "this is Edward Johnson—a client of mine from Volunteer Space. Mr. Johnson, this is my father."

I stand and nod to him but keep my distance.

"Mr. Johnson is an alcoholic," she says. "He hasn't had a drink in twelve days. He called me about an urge he's having tonight, and I invited him over to talk it through."

"That's right," I say, looking humble, hanging my head.

Miller calms down. He seems like a good guy. I decide to push my luck a little.

"It's an honor to meet you, Mr. Miller. I agree with just about every stand you've taken."

"Hot damn," he says. "That's what I like to hear. What's your name again?"

"Eddy, sir."

"I've just come from a campaign meeting. Plotting the final stretch…"

"Daddy, Mr. Johnson and I were just finishing up. He needs to go home so he can get up in the morning for work. So don't you start in with your silly politics."

"Hell, Peg. I never get to meet regular people. I'm so sick and tired of talking to experts."

"Mr. Johnson is tired."

"Maybe you could call in sick tomorrow, Eddy."

"I don't know. They might really need me."

"Tell you what," he says. "How about this?" He pulls a money clip from his pants pocket, peels a hundred-dollar bill loose, and holds it up. "For one hour of your time."

He hands me the hundred. I put it away.

"Believe me, there's no need to give him money," Peggy Miller says.

"Hell, it doesn't look like he has any of his own. Have you seen his truck? Maybe you should run along now, Peg. Me and Eddy are just going to jaw a little."

"Oh, all right. But don't keep him long."

"Sure thing, darlin'." He kisses her on the cheek.

"And don't give him any more money."

She reaches out to shake my hand. "Good evening, Mr. Johnson," she says. "Call me, please, tomorrow morning. I would like to talk with you some more about our friend Maria."

"Sure thing," I say. She lets herself out.

Miller and I listen to the sound of her loafers crossing the foyer.

"So," he says, turning to face me with a big smile. "You like liquor, do you?"

"Yes, sir."

"Call me Big Frank."

"Big Frank."

"Eddy, let me tell you something. These do-gooders mean well, but they don't know where to stop. Now and then, any of us could use a little help. There's nothing wrong with that. But once you're back on your feet, you need to stand tall—walk through this world knowing what you want and grabbing hold of it. Hell, Peggy's a great kid and all, but damn."

"The drinking has been a problem for me..."

"Maybe you'd like a belt or two right now."

"Oh, I don't know."

He goes to a table against one of the walls and opens a drawer. He pulls out a pint of Johnnie Walker Black. "Have a seat, Eddy," he says. I sit on one of the leather sofas, and he comes and sits across from me. He breaks the seal on the pint and offers me the first drink.

"You're a good man, Big Frank," I say. I take a swig and hand him the bottle. He gulps down twice what I did.

"Hot dog! Don't that feel good?"

"Yes, it does."

We both drink some more, then leave the bottle sitting on the table between us.

"So, tell me," he says. "Did you see the debate?"

"I did."

"What did you think?"

"Oh, you won, no question. You were so sure of yourself, and he seemed nervous. He was sweating the whole time."

"Yeah, I fixed it so there were a couple extra spotlights on him." He laughs, slapping his knee. "It's a wonder he didn't end up microwaved."

He drinks some more and so do I.

"They had that debate rigged start to finish—two minutes for this, one minute for that, and so many rules—like instead of facing off we were waltzing around. I had half a mind to walk over and punch him in the face. Break his goddamn nose on live TV. Bad idea according to the experts, but hell, if you got to choose between two men—I don't care if it's for mayor or hunting buddy or whatever—you're gonna pick the one who can knock the other one down. If the public doesn't like a man who throws a punch during a debate—so what? They're sure as hell not going to vote for the guy who gets his nose broke and has to be helped offstage."

We finish the bottle.

"I should have followed my instincts on that one. The polls say I won the debate, but hell, I like doing things *my* way."

He gets up, goes back to the table, opens the drawer, and pulls out another pint of Johnnie Walker Black.

"Eddy, I do believe we are going to get ourselves a little drunk."

CHAPTER II

IT'S MAYBE TWO O'CLOCK when I let myself in my room. I turn on the light. The guy sitting on my bed doesn't like that. He's got used to the dark and now he has to squint. All the same, he's got me covered, a big pistol pointed at my stomach.

"Don't even breathe," he says. With his other hand he reaches in his jacket and pulls out a pair of dark sunglasses. He puts them on.

He's a nasty-looking thug, big and blunt in a cheap suit that doesn't fit. He's got a couple scars on his ugly face, and a bulb of a nose that's been broken, smashed, and flattened plenty. He's the kind of guy who doesn't cost much and never did.

"Up," he says, gesturing with the gun.

I lift my hands on either side of my head.

My room is all topsy-turvy. I'm pretty much a slob, but it never looked this bad. Boxes of books have been pulled open and dumped on the floor. My dresser and closet are empty, clothes strewn everywhere. The mattress has been slashed open like the belly of a fish, its stuffing pulled out in tufts.

"I get it," I tell the guy. "You must be the new maid."

"Cute," he says.

"I keep telling them in housekeeping to stop hiring psychopaths."

"Be real peaceful and pay attention," he says. "Something you should know about me. I don't like to repeat myself."

"Well, did you find what you were looking for?"

"If I did, I wouldn't still be here."

"What *are* you looking for?"

"The Arnold. What else?"

"The Arnold? What makes you think I have it?"

"I know for a fact you do. So can the charade and hand it over."

"I never even saw the book. I'm assuming Maria Juarez has it."

"No, you bought it from Maria at the warehouse. Then you shot your gun to scare off the chauffeur. You double-crossed Peggy Miller, and maybe you're thinking so far so good. But now it's over. You're going to give the book to me."

"Maria wasn't at the warehouse."

"Yeah, and this gun ain't loaded," he says, calling my attention to it again.

"You've got it all wrong," I say.

"Oh yeah?" Without looking away from me or moving the gun, he reaches around behind his big rump and pats at the mattress, searching for something. He finds it.

"Well now," he says. "What do we have here?"

It's one of my Faulkners. The bastard's got his ugly paws on one of my Faulkners.

"What do you know?" he says. "A near mint first of *As I Lay Dying*."

"Leave it alone."

"How much is this baby worth, Johnson?"

"Leave it alone."

"How much?"

"Four hundred dollars."

"And without the dust jacket?"

"I've got a buyer for that book."

"Without the dust jacket, it's worth eighty, maybe a hundred bucks. That's weird, how so much of the value is in the dust jacket. They say don't judge a book by its cover…"

"I don't have the Arnold," I say.

He sets the Faulkner next to him on the bed and slips a finger inside the dust jacket.

"Hey! Come on!" I say.

He rips the dust jacket in two.

"You scumbag," I say. "You got no idea what you're doing."

"Oh?"

"I've got friends. I'm connected."

"Sure you are. A jerk like you."

He reaches around and finds another book. It's my *Walden*. *Holy shit!*

"All right," I say in a hurry. "All right. I've got the Arnold."

He puts the *Walden* down.

"That's more like it."

"It's not here. I got it stashed somewhere."

"Where?"

"A guy's holding it for me."

He stands, leaving the *Walden* on the bed.

"Let's go get it."

"I can't. This is a heavy guy. I can't bother him tonight."

"One of your so-called connections?" he says, sneering. "Okay, here's the deal, Johnson. You got till tomorrow to turn it over. You be here, with the book, by two p.m. You play it straight, you walk away nice and easy. Understand?"

"No problem. Just don't hurt any more of my books."

"Okay, turn around." He gestures with the gun. "Put your hands against the wall."

I get one last good look at him—one of his scars, on his left cheek, is shaped like an *L*—then I face the wall and put my hands against it.

He steps up behind me. I feel his gun nuzzling my lower back, and I smell his breath. A big hand—the one that ruined my Faulkner—reaches around, finds my gun, and takes it.

"Tomorrow, Johnson," he says.

There's an explosion on the top of my head, my starting to scream, then nothing.

CHAPTER 12

I WAKE UP lying on the worn-out floorboards of my room. The top of my head—where I got hit—is swollen and hurts like hell. My eyes hurt from the sunlight coming in the window. I must be hungover too. I squint at my watch. It's nine-thirty.

After a while I get off the floor. I go in the bathroom. I strip and get in the shower and let the water run over me a long time. I get out of the shower, dry off, rub a toothbrush around in my mouth, stick some deodorant under my arms.

Back in my room, I step into a pair of pants. I put some other things on. I pour some bourbon in my glass and sit on the bed. The damaged Faulkner is next to me. I hardly glance at it. I shove it away behind me so I don't have to see it. I sip at the bourbon and look around at the disaster my room is. It looks like the inside of my head.

I think of a ditty my father would sing with me on his knee:

Another day, another deal.
Otherwise no bed, no meal.

It doesn't matter how you feel.
Another day, another deal.

My father. His trouble was he never knew the difference between a good deal and a bad one. All his life selling encyclopedias door-to-door. With his *Readers' Digest Condensed Books* enshrined in the den, his subscription to *Buried Treasure!*, his shoeboxes full of clippings from *Parade* and *TV Guide*. At his funeral, as they lowered him into the hole, all I could think about was how he threw away my comic book collection. A whole foot-locker full of ten and twelve centers in mint condition.

When I come down the stairs to the lobby, Mrs. Nelson—the manager of the Alamo Boardinghouse—is standing behind the counter.

"Mr. Johnson," she says, calling me over. "I hope you're ready to pay your rent in full right here and now. Yesterday was the fifth."

"Don't worry. I've got your money."

"I mean it. I'll toss you and your stuff out of here so fast it'll make your head spin."

I walk to the counter.

She says, "This is the third month in a row you've been late." Her voice is like a foghorn.

"Keep quiet," I say. I yank my wallet, pull two hundreds out, and drop them on the counter. Mrs. Nelson examines the bills closely, holding them up to the light before stuffing them in her bra.

My truck is parked across the street. I walk to it and get in. Fumbling around in the center console, I find a pair of sunglasses and put them on. That helps a little. I tell myself, *One thing at a time.*

I need a gun.

I start my truck and pull away from the curb into traffic. I work my way north. By ten-thirty, I'm way out on Burnet Road, past Koening.

I turn into the parking lot of the River City Gun Mart.

I pull around to the drive-through, stopping next to the big sign that lists the stuff for sale.

The intercom in the sign crackles a little. "Your order please," a man's voice says.

"Yeah," I say, leaning out the window of my truck toward the intercom. "I need a Smith and Wesson snub nose .38, hold the holster."

"Would you like some ammunition with that, sir?"

"No."

"All right," the guy says. "One Smith and Wesson snub nose .38, no holster. That will be two hundred dollars. Drive through please."

I pull up to the window and give the guy my driver's license. When he gives it back to me, I hand him two hundreds. He reaches the gun out to me.

I pull into a parking space. I get a box of ammo from the glove compartment, load the gun, and put it in my holster.

CHAPTER 13

TWENTY MINUTES LATER, I'm back downtown, heading south on Nueches toward the river. I turn off on 2nd Street, where railroad tracks crisscross the pavement and there are still some warehouses.

A few blocks east, I pull into a visitor spot in front of Romano Brothers Books, a wholesale operation in a big brick warehouse. There are green Romano Brothers trucks parked along both sides of the street. A couple trucks are backed up to loading docks. One of Joey's guys—I've seen him around but don't know his name—is sitting on a chair outside the visitor's entrance flipping through a magazine.

I get out of my truck and walk toward him.

"Heya," he says, looking up. "What's poppin'?"

"I'm here to see Joey."

"You're Johnson. Right?"

I nod.

"Go ahead. He's in his office."

"Thanks," I say.

I pull the door open and step into a little waiting room with some chairs and a rack of magazines. There's a receptionist's desk but no one behind it. I walk down the hall to Joey's office. The door is cracked open. I say, "Joey? You in there?"

"Come on in," he says.

I push the door open and see Joey at his desk.

He's a handsome guy with dark hair and blue-green eyes. He's trim and tanned. Joey takes care of himself. Gets manicures, has a guy come in to shine his shoes. He's got a silk shirt on and plenty of gold around his neck and fingers.

He's eating Chinese out of Styrofoam containers. He looks up and sees me in the doorway.

"Eddy!" he says. He swivels away from his desk, wiping his hands on a napkin. "Eddy! Long time no see."

He stands and comes toward me. He grabs the back of my neck and gives me a playful shake. "You crazy bastard. I was saying to Rollo just the other day, *How come Eddy don't come around?*" He pulls me close, and we hug. He gives my shoulder a squeeze, then lets me go. It's like being left alone by a bear.

"I hate to bother you," I say.

"You hate to bother me? What are you talking about? Do I look bothered?"

I laugh a little.

He shuts the office door.

"Have a seat," he says. I sit in a chair in front of his desk. "You want a drink?"

"Sure."

He makes some noise behind me where there's a fridge, and he hands me a glass with ice in it. A bottle of Chivas is within reach on the desk. I pour some.

Joey sits down and goes back to his lunch. I sip the scotch and watch him eat.

"How's Frankie?" I say.

"I just got a letter from him. He's okay. He gets out in April."

"I thought he still had two years."

"He got parole."

Frankie Romano. Not as level-headed as his big brother Joey. He got busted a year back for a truck hijacking—a semi full of Simon and Schuster nabbed in the middle of the night at a phony roadblock somewhere in Arkansas. Frankie wrecked the truck and got caught.

Joey finishes eating and dumps the Styrofoam in the trash can. He tilts his chair back.

"Eddy, you don't look good."

"I've got a problem."

"Money? How much you need?"

"No, Joey. Nothing like that. I've got some guy messing with me. I don't even know him. He was in my room when I got home last night, looking for a book he thinks I got. He was waving a .38 around, saying to give him the book or else."

"You don't know him?"

"He's a big guy. Ugly. Got a scar like an *L* on his left cheek. A nose that's been broke plenty."

Joey thinks. "Doesn't ring a bell," he says. "One of the boys might know him. I'll check it out. Is he working for somebody?"

"He must be. I don't know who."

"What's the book?"

"*Dear Sweet Texas* by Arnold."

Joey whistles. "How'd you get your hands on that?"

"I didn't. I don't have it."

"But he thinks you've got it…"

"He turned my room inside out looking for it. Then, when I showed up, he started defacing my books, trying to convince me to hand it over."

"Oh. A tough guy," Joey says.

"Yeah. And when he left, he banged me on the head with his piece."

Joey makes me lean forward so he can feel the bump. He whistles again. Then he pushes an intercom button on his phone and says, "Rollo, come in here. Bring Artie and Sal."

"Eddy," he says. "I'm glad you came to me. I owe you a favor, and now I'm going to do this for you. Relax. That guy won't bother you again. He wants to play rough, he'll get his share."

There's a knock on the door.

"Yeah," Joey calls.

The door opens and in come three of the biggest, meanest-looking guys I've ever seen. They've got thick necks, wide, square faces without expression, and eyes like you'd see on a shark—cold and steady. The smallest of them has trouble squeezing in through the doorway. Together—standing around awkwardly—they fill the little office with their bulk and the smell of their colognes. They're all wearing suits.

I know Rollo. The favor I'm collecting on is an alibi I made good for Frankie and Rollo the night they torched a little porno shop on South Lamar. The other two guys I've never seen.

"Heya, boss," they all say.

"Have a cigar, boys." They reach out as Joey passes the box around. They put the cigars in their jacket pockets.

"Boys, I got a little job for you. Any of you know a guy who's got a scar like an *L* on his left cheek? His nose is all messed up. Big guy."

"I know that guy," Rollo says.

"Packs a .38."

"Yeah, that's him."

"Is he connected?"

"No. He hires out. He was asking me for work. I think he said he done some things for Capitol City Books."

"Those bastards."

"That was two, three weeks ago."

"Well, last night he messed up big time. He got out of line and roughed up a friend of mine. Eddy here. Rollo, you know Eddy."

Rollo nods to me.

"This here's Artie and Sal." They nod too.

Joey says to Rollo, "You find this guy. He's dead. Nobody hits a pal of Joey Romano's on the head and gets away with it."

"Maybe you could just tell him to lay off," I say.

"Eddy. Relax, will ya? Have another drink."

"But I need to know who he's working for."

"Right. Okay, boys. Listen up. If you got to off the guy, make him tell you who he works for first."

"You got it, boss," Sal says.

"Rollo, keep them in line, okay? I don't need a mess like that thing on Red River."

"Sure thing, boss."

"Okay, boys." Joey stands. He goes and opens the door, slaps each of them on the back as they file out. Then he shuts the door, goes back to his desk, and sits.

"See, Eddy?" he says. "No problem."

"I appreciate it, Joey."

"I got to say though, Eddy. I can't help but notice. The only time you come see me is when you have a problem. Everything's okay, you're a stranger. You kind of hurt my feelings."

"Maybe I should have come around more, Joey. Showed how much I care… But you were always on my mind," I say, half-singing. "You were always on my mind…"

Joey laughs.

"There you go," he says. "That's the old Eddy. Don't be so serious."

"Sometimes I think I'll quit this stinking racket."

"And do what?"

"I don't know. It's just I get worn down. Not like when I was younger. Maybe I ought to get a regular job, like in a library."

"Oh yeah, sure. You'd last about three weeks. You're a book dealer, Eddy."

"I know, I know."

"Go home and relax. Take it easy. Keep drinking till the bump on your head goes down. I'll let you know about this guy. If they bring him in alive, maybe you'd like to talk to him."

"That'd be great."

Joey holds out his hand. I kiss his ring.

CHAPTER 14

I DRIVE NORTH SIX BLOCKS and park in front of Joe Bob's Grille. Before I go in, I walk to the corner to buy a paper at Pappy's kiosk.

Pappy's behind the window chewing on the unlit stump of a cheap cigar.

"Well, well, if it ain't Eddy Johnson," he says.

I grab a paper and hand him a quarter. I fold the paper and put it under my arm.

"Hey, Eddy," Pappy says, waving me in closer. He takes the cigar out of his mouth and leans forward, almost through the window, resting his forearms on a stack of *Dallas Times Heralds*. "Hey, Eddy. Heard you spent a lot of money on a cab last night."

"Yeah?"

"Way out on the east side, the way I heard it. Got out there okay, but you needed a ride to get back to town."

"What of it?"

"Nothing. Nothing at all." He smiles, showing his rotten teeth. "Only maybe if I heard it, some other folks heard it too."

"Like who?"

"Like maybe a couple of toughs who've been asking around about a guy they ran into on the east side last night—a guy who can see in the dark and has a nervous driver."

"Who's been asking?" I say.

"One of them had a hole in his leg."

"Who?" I say.

Pappy puts the cigar back in his mouth. "Thirty bucks," he says.

"No way."

"Twenty bucks."

"Forget it."

"Okay, ten bucks. But you got to buy a couple magazines."

"Five bucks," I say.

He shakes his head no.

"That's okay. I'll find out some other way." I turn and start walking up the sidewalk.

Pappy leans even farther out his window. "You cheap bastard!" he shouts after me.

I keep walking.

"You pissed off the wrong people, Eddy. You'll see."

I go on into Joe Bob's. The place is deserted. I go to the counter and sit on a stool.

The waitress sticks her face in the service window.

"Yeah?" she says.

"Coffee. And—how's the chili?"

"What, are you kidding?" she says.

She comes around, pours me a mug of coffee.

"Give me the chili," I say. "Can I use the phone?"

"Yeah, sure. Whatever." She goes in the kitchen.

I drink some coffee and go behind the counter to the phone. I dial the Millers' number. I copied it off the phone in their den last night in case it was unlisted.

Peggy Miller answers. I say, "This is Eddy Johnson."

"Yes?" she says.

"Have you heard from Maria?"

"No. Why would I?"

"She still has the book."

"Look, Mr. Johnson. I don't know what kind of game you're playing. You should be ashamed of yourself. Give me Daddy's book back."

"I don't have it."

"I happen to know that you do."

"Right. Because of the goon who came by my room last night?"

"I don't know anything about that."

"Yeah? Well, we're wasting time. You don't trust me? Okay. Fine."

"Why should I?"

"If you knew anything about the book business, you'd know it wouldn't do me any good to steal the Arnold. There'd be no point. As rare as it is, I'd never be able to sell it."

"So you're saying Maria still has it?"

"Sure. She's probably scared, lying low somewhere. If I can find her before those thugs from the warehouse do, I can still buy the book from her."

She's thinking.

"What do you have to lose?" I say.

"Well, she hasn't called me."

"Do you know her address?"

She hesitates, then says, "All right. I'll tell you. Hold the line please." She puts the phone down and goes off.

The waitress comes in from the kitchen with a bowl of chili. She puts it on the counter next to my newspaper and goes back into the kitchen.

Then Peggy Miller is on the line. She says, "Maria Juarez lives at 318 Clawson Road."

"Thanks," I say. "And hey. Level with me. You sent that guy by my room, didn't you?"

"I did nothing of the kind."

"If it wasn't you, then it must have been Bart Robinson."

"You leave Barty out of this," she says.

"Barty?"

She says, "You are mistaken, Mr. Johnson. Mr. Robinson has nothing to do with any of this."

"Okay. But remember, if I get the book, you owe me four hundred dollars."

"Goodbye, Mr. Johnson."

She hangs up. I do too.

There's a phone book. In the Yellow Pages—under *Books; Rare, Dealers*—I find *B. Robinson, Exclusive Texana. By appointment only.* There's no address.

I dial the number.

There are some rings, then a woman's voice says, "Mr. Robinson's office. This is Sheila. How may I help you?"

"Put Bart Robinson on the line," I say.

"Who shall I tell him is calling?"

"Tell him it's Billy Joe Mortimer."

"And you wish to speak with Mr. Robinson concerning…"

"Books," I say. "He buys books, don't he? Books about Texas?"

"Have you ever done business with Mr. Robinson?" she says.

"No. I got his number out of the Yellow Pages. I don't handle books much. See, I've got this pawn shop—Quick Cash Pawn, on East 6th Street."

"Sir, it is not likely that any books you have would be of interest to Mr. Robinson. He handles only the—"

"It's just one book," I say. "*Dear Sweet Texas.*"

"By Arnold?"

"Right."

"By Herman Arnold?"

"Right," I say. "Herman Arnold. Is it worth anything? Looks like it's autographed."

"It is probably not worth much. It's quite common. Mr. Robinson has several of them, all autographed."

"Maybe he'd like another one. I don't have much in it."

"How did you acquire it?"

"Some Mexican gal brought it into the pawn shop. How much can you give me for it?"

"Sir, I am going to put you through to Mr. Robinson. I'm certain, though, that he will insist on seeing the book before making an offer. If he happens to have an interest in it."

"Put him on," I say.

There's a click, a full minute of silence, then another click. A man's voice says, "This is Bart Robinson."

"Bart, my name is Billy Joe Mortimer. I own Quick Cash Pawn, over on East 6th Street. This morning a young Mexican gal—"

"Yes," Robinson says. "Miss Easton has told me your

particulars. The book you have is common and not worth much. Still, if it is in mint condition, I will make you a reasonable offer."

"How much?" I say.

"In excellent condition: perhaps two hundred dollars."

"I knew it!" I say. "Two hundred dollars!"

"If you bring it to my office this afternoon, I would be prepared to pay you in cash."

"Yes, sir! Where are you?"

"My office is on the twentieth floor of the Sherman Building." The most exclusive of the fancy new high-rises downtown. It overlooks the river and has a helipad on its roof. "I am only here until two o'clock. Can you make it by then?"

"You betcha. I'll be there."

"And remember, Mr. Mortimer. The condition the book is in is of paramount importance. Please be careful with it."

"I will."

"Goodbye," Robinson says, and we hang up.

It's one o'clock.

I go around the counter to my stool and sit. I start in on the chili, making with the free saltines.

CHAPTER 15

I PARK MY TRUCK in the basement of the Sherman Building and take an elevator up to the twentieth floor. It's a smooth, quick ride. Under my arm—inside a brown grocery bag that's folded flat—I'm carrying a hardback P. G. Wodehouse novel worth five dollars. It's about the same size as *Dear Sweet Texas*.

When the elevator doors open, I step out into a modern, brightly lit corridor. A directory on the wall reads *B. Robinson, suite 2028*. I walk until I get to a door with that number. I open it and walk into a small reception area.

A woman—Sheila, I presume, who answered the phone when I called—is sitting behind a desk. She's in her thirties, distinguished, a string of pearls around her neck.

She's saying into the phone, "I'm sorry. Mr. Robinson's price on that particular item is not negotiable."

She smiles at me, motions for me to sit in one of the chairs.

"But sir, that is the volume's only flaw. A minor one in our opinion. And in mint condition it is valued at seventeen hundred dollars."

"Is Mr. Robinson in?" I say.

"One moment please," she says to the guy on the phone. She puts him on hold and says, "Are you Mr. Mortimer?"

"That's right." I tap the bag under my arm.

She says, "Mr. Robinson is expecting you. You may go in." She points to a door.

"Thanks," I say. I go to the door, open it, and step inside a huge office. Real swanky. One whole wall is floor to ceiling glass: a panorama of the river to the south, the wooded rise of hills beyond. In the distance I can see the rusted scaffolding of the neon Genie Car Wash sign on South Lamar.

There's a desk at the far end of the office, maybe thirty yards away. Behind it is a fat man in his fifties or sixties, pale and balding. He's wearing a silk suit. I walk to the desk.

"Mr. Mortimer?" he says without getting up.

"In the flesh," I say.

He points to the grocery bag. "And this must be the book you've come to sell." He reaches for it, but I don't hand it over. I step back.

"Mr. Mortimer, please. I will need to examine the volume in order to make you an offer."

"You already know what shape it's in," I say. "And my name isn't Mortimer." I pull the pistol out and point it at him. "It's Eddy Johnson."

"Ah," he says, smiling. "How clever of you. How enterprising."

"Keep your hands on top of the desk," I say.

"Certainly. Can I assume that you've come to thank me for referring you?"

"You don't even know me."

"No," he says. "I am sadly—or rather, happily—out of touch with the streets. When a person such as yourself became necessary, I called George Delaney. He gave me your name."

"Delaney recommended me?" Delaney runs the Austin Book Show.

"He told me you would be inexpensive and reliable."

"What's your angle?"

Robinson laughs. "I don't have an angle, Mr. Johnson. I've simply done a favor for the daughter of a good client. Frank Miller has spent a lot of money with me over the years. When his daughter called and asked me to refer someone such as yourself, I obliged. Free of charge."

"And offered her the use of your warehouse."

"Not mine," he says. "I was a tenant there some years ago. I might have mentioned it to her."

"And when she called you again—late last night, to tell you the deal fell through—you hired someone else. The cheap thug that searched my room and roughed me up."

"You can hardly take that personally, Mr. Johnson. The book is worth twenty thousand dollars."

"The bump on my head I take personally. Also, the first edition *As I Lay Dying* your pal defaced trying to make me talk."

"I certainly in no way represented to the person in question that—"

"Plus he took my gun. I had to go buy this one."

"I am certain we can settle these petty differences, Mr. Johnson. You will find me more than reasonable. I am sorry this affair has worked out so badly for you."

"The way I see it, you owe me nine hundred dollars. Three

for the gun and six for the Faulkner."

"I will gladly give you the money you want," Robinson says. Holding his jacket open so I can see, he reaches inside his breast pocket and gets his wallet out. He counts nine hundreds onto the desk and puts his wallet away. He hands me the money.

"And now," he says, "if there is nothing further, I think you should leave."

I pocket the money.

"But there is something further," I say. "There's the four hundred dollars Peggy Miller still owes me, due upon receipt of the book."

"You'll need to take that up with her."

"I'm not handing the book over unless I get paid. She'll reimburse you."

"Oh, all right," he says. He gets his wallet out and pulls four hundreds from it. He hands them to me.

"Thanks," I say, putting the money away.

I put the bag with the Wodehouse in it on his desk. "To Miss Peggy Miller, with my compliments," I say. "Pleasure doing business with you."

"I'm only glad it's over," he says. "I'm glad the book is back where it belongs."

"There's something else," I say. "Assuming you might be talking with that thug sometime soon, you might do him a favor. You could tell him he should have listened when I said I was connected. I've told friends of mine what he did and they're out looking for him."

"Of course," Robinson says. "Likewise, if you are, as you say, connected, you will kindly tell your friends that you and I have resolved our differences and have nothing more to do with each other."

"Sure thing, Barty."

That ruffles him.

"Get out," he says, pointing to the door. "Get the hell out."

"All right, don't worry, I'm going…Barty."

He starts to get up, but I lift the pistol and he stops.

He says, "I should have known better than to stoop—even for a moment—to the level of scum like you."

"You can wash your hands after I leave," I say. I back over to the door, my pistol still pointed at him.

I open the door and go through it. Sheila, behind her desk, isn't on the phone. She sees the gun in my hand, says, "Oh my God!" and puts her hands up. Her eyes are big with fear.

"It's okay," I say. "Take it easy."

I go to the entrance, put the pistol away, and step out into the corridor. Nobody's around. I walk to the elevators. One of them is waiting with open doors. I go inside and push the button marked *G* for garage.

CHAPTER 16

DEEP IN THE EAST SIDE. Clawson Road runs north-south, a country lane of a road—narrow, with no curbs or sidewalks. Its crumbling pavement winds through a part of town caught between airport flightpaths and the stink of a nearby landfill. Big trees line the street, dappling it with shade, cedar elms and gnarled burr oaks. The houses are shotgun shacks crowded close together. There are healthy vegetable gardens and here and there some chickens.

Maria's house is like a lot of them. It's got a tin roof and a small yard of hard-packed dirt. A pecan tree next to the house has some of its branches propped up with two-by-fours. In front, where a curb would be, there's a Pontiac four-door on cinderblocks. I pull up behind the Pontiac and get out of my truck.

There's no sign of life except an old man asleep on the porch of the house next to Maria's. All around me are the smells of home cooking. And there's a car that bothers me. Parked ahead of the Pontiac. It's a fairly new Delta 88. Its engine is running but no one's in it.

I walk into Maria's yard. I'm about twenty feet from the front door when it opens and out comes a big guy carrying a kid—a boy, maybe ten years old, fighting and kicking for all he's worth.

The guy's too busy to notice me. He's grabbing for arms and legs that keep slipping free. He's red in the face and breathing heavy. But the other guy, the second one through the door, doesn't see anything but me. I recognize him in a flash—the way he's tall and narrow in the doorway. It's the guy I shot in the warehouse. He's holding a gun. He points it at me and shoots.

Behind me, the windshield of the Pontiac explodes. I leap at the Pontiac—rolling across its hood on bits of broken glass, hearing the second shot and the bullet ripping through the hood's metal just behind me. I land on my back on the other side, in the road, and bounce into a crouch, my gun in hand.

"Drop it," the guy says. Even with his bad leg, he's already made it around the back end of the Pontiac, and he has his gun pointed at me. A profile shot.

I drop the gun.

"Now stand," he says. "Nice and slow."

I do that.

"You're the guy who shot me last night," he says. "Johnson. I been looking for you."

"I'm sorry I shot you. I was just trying to warn you—let you know I had a gun."

I hear the other guy and the kid behind me, still going at it, making their way to the Delta.

"Give me a break," I say. "It was an accident."

"It's the last one you'll ever have. We're gonna take you for a ride. I'm gonna spend some time on you. Kick that gun over here."

I kick the gun, and it goes off.

The guy who's got me covered flies backward, landing flat on the road, his own gun gone—clattering to a stop near my truck. He's moaning.

I go after my gun, get it, and whirl to face the other guy. He lets the kid go and puts his hands in the air.

"Please," he says. "Please. Don't shoot me." He's a tough guy, but he doesn't know I'm only lucky with a gun. He's not used to fear, and it doesn't suit him.

The kid, when his feet hit the ground, runs over and gets behind me.

"Shoot him!" he says. "Shoot him in his fat head!"

I say, "Shut up, you little pipsqueak. Beat it."

The kid goes off, back to the house.

"Who are you working for?" I say to the big guy.

"The Capalettis."

"The Capalettis?!" I'm going around town shooting guys who are connected to the Capalettis? Nobody messes with them. They run a wholesale operation—Capaletti and Son Books—out of a warehouse near South 17th and Oltorf. They've got a deal with the Romanos. The Capalettis keep south of the river, the Romanos north. And everyone else keeps out of the way.

"That's Franco Capaletti," the big guy says, meaning the guy who's lying in the street moaning, another of my bullets in him. Franco Capaletti, as in *and son*. Pappy wasn't kidding about me pissing off the wrong people.

"Damn," I say. "Come on, let's help him."

We go to Franco. He's lying on his side curled up, clutching his gun hand. It's bloody. I must have shot his gun right out of it.

The big guy helps him to his feet. When he's up, he shoves the big guy away and, staggering to get his balance, faces me alone. What a mess he is. He looks terrible—pale, trembling, all bloody. There's the bulk of a bandage wrapped around his left thigh under his pants. "Kill me," he says. "You punk. Go ahead."

"I'm so sorry, Mr. Capaletti. I've got no quarrel with you. I didn't even know who you were till your pal told me just now."

"Spare me the shame and kill me now." He takes a step toward me, then faints. He goes all the way down, banging his head on the street and lying still.

"Here," I tell the big guy. "I'll help you get him in the car."

I grab Franco under the knees, the big guy gets his armpits, and we carry him to the Delta. I free up one hand and open the door. We lift Franco in.

"Get him to a doctor," I say. "And listen. Tell Old Man Capaletti I've got nothing but respect for him and his family."

"You got a funny way of showing it, though. If I was you, I might think about getting out of town for a while."

"Maybe I should."

"That sure is some fancy shooting, though. I've never seen anything like it."

"Just tell Luigi I'm sorry. Okay?"

"I'll tell him." He gets behind the wheel of the Delta and races off.

CHAPTER 17

I HOLSTER MY GUN and look around. The old man is gone from the porch. Franco's gun is still in the road. I pick it up. It's a .38 like mine but with a longer barrel. I put it under the seat in my truck and walk to Maria's house.

The front door is ajar. I push on it and step into a living room. There's hardly any furniture and nothing on the walls. It has the charm of a dental clinic.

The kid is sitting on an orange sofa drinking a can of Dr. Pepper, pulling potato chips from a big bag. He looks over at me and rolls his eyes.

I shut the front door behind me.

"What do *you* want?" he says.

"I need to talk to Maria."

"Not gonna happen."

"Come on. I did you a favor. Where is she?" He ignores me. "You little twerp."

That gets his attention. He says, "I am not a twerp. And I'm not a pipsqueak either. I don't take crap off anybody."

"You were taking plenty off those guys until I showed up."

"I would have got out of that. Besides, all you did was have some dumb luck."

"So what? The main thing is it worked out for both of us. I don't know where those guys were taking you, but I don't think it was to get ice cream. It seems obvious to me we're on the same side."

"I guess so," the kid says.

I sit on a matching armchair.

"You want some potato chips?" he says, holding the bag out.

"No, I want to talk to Maria."

"I don't even know you."

"I'm from the Millers. Peggy Miller hired me to go to the warehouse last night. I'm still looking to buy the book."

"It's the *book* you're after?"

"Sure. What else? Isn't that why those two goons were here?"

"They want the photographs."

"What photographs?"

The kid says, "Mister, you don't know nothin'."

"What photographs?"

"The ones in the book. Stuck between some pages. Dirty photographs of Miller and some woman. They didn't tell you?"

"I don't think they even know you have them, kid. Peggy Miller got Maria's note and never told her father. She thinks she's just buying the book."

"Why would she pay five hundred dollars for that stupid book?"

"It's worth a lot more than that. It's collectible. There were only two hundred copies printed, and most of those are probably destroyed."

"If it was the only copy in the world, I wouldn't give you ten cents for it. I looked at it for about a minute. It's pathetic."

"It's not my kind of book. But to Texana collectors, it's considered a gem."

"Whatever. If you want the book for five hundred dollars, you can have it."

"What about the photographs?"

"Those are two thousand. But we got a special going: buy the photographs, we throw in the book."

"Two thousand… Is that what the Capalettis offered?"

"I don't know about any Capalettis. This is Romano territory."

"You be sure and remind them of that the next time they come by for a playdate. That guy I shot was Franco Capaletti."

"For real?"

"Yes. And they were at the warehouse last night."

"They're working for the mayor."

"The mayor? What's he got to do with this?"

"Maria called him. It was my idea. All along, Maria wanted to make the photos public. But she was going to give them to the newspaper. For nothing. And we couldn't afford to do that. So we decided to sell them to the Millers. But then I thought maybe I could sell them to the mayor instead."

"That's pretty slick, kid. I'm impressed."

He likes that. "Thanks," he says. "And the mayor really went for it. He offered us two thousand dollars. He was supposed to send some aides at six o'clock last night with the cash."

"But then the Capalettis showed up…"

"They busted in here about five-thirty. Maria and I got away with the photos and the book. But we left behind a note with the address of the warehouse and when the meeting was. When we got home, the note was gone."

"That explains why they were waiting for me at the warehouse. They gave me pretty much the same treatment they gave you and Maria."

"I totally screwed things up. We should have just taken the five hundred dollars."

"Don't be so hard on yourself."

"But it went all wrong…"

"Just a couple details. The main thing is you took a shot. You came close to quadrupling your money. How old are you, anyway?"

"Ten."

"What's your name?"

"Raoul."

"So *you're* Raoul. Pleased to meet you. I'm Eddy. Eddy Johnson. I'm a book dealer."

He puts his little hand up and we high five.

"How'd Maria know about the photographs?"

"Miller would call her into his library sometimes and get fresh with her. He'd chase her around the library tables, fondle her if he got the chance. He'd run out of breath, then he'd give her fifty bucks and send her back to the pantry. One time, about a week before she got fired, he took the photos out of the book in the glass display case and made Maria look at them. The filthy scum."

"Listen, kid. I can see why Maria did what she did."

"They fired her with no notice."

"I understand her wanting to stick it to Miller. But listen, this situation is out of hand. We need to get the book and photos back to the Millers as soon as possible."

"I guess you're right."

"I've got five hundred dollars with me. Let's just do the original deal."

"The stuff isn't here."

There's a loud knock on the door. I motion for Raoul to keep quiet and I get my gun out.

"You in the house!" a man's voice says. "Come out with your hands up!"

And I realize: it's cops. Someone must have reported the shooting.

CHAPTER 18

I LOOK OUT A WINDOW and see a patrol car parked behind my truck.

"It's the police," I tell Raoul.

"You've got one minute," a cop outside the front door says.

I put my gun away.

"I'm coming out! Don't shoot!" I yank my wallet, pull out a hundred-dollar bill and one of my business cards. I hand them to Raoul.

"If I get arrested, I'll be out tomorrow morning at the latest. Just keep trying my number. We've got to do this deal."

He nods.

I open the door and step out onto the porch, my hands up.

"Freeze," a cop says. A pistol pokes the small of my back. Someone's hands reach around, find my gun, and take it.

"Has it been fired?" the cop says.

I turn around some to look at the cops. I recognize the one with his pistol against my spine: Jones. I've seen him around. The other cop I don't know. His tag says Wilkins. He's sniffing my gun.

"Yep. It's been fired, all right."

Jones says, "Who else is in the house?"

"Nobody. A kid."

"Is he armed?"

"No, he's just a little kid."

"Put cuffs on him, Wilkins," Jones says. "I'm gonna check it out."

Wilkins cuffs my hands.

"You in the house!" Jones shouts. "Come out with your hands up! This is the police!"

He stands next to the open door, his pistol ready.

Raoul comes to the door holding his can of Dr. Pepper.

"Is there anyone else inside, kid?"

"Just me."

Jones puts his piece away. "What's going on here?"

"Nothing much. *The Flintstones* are about to come on."

"Jesus," Jones says. He turns to me. "Yours?"

I shake my head no.

Jones looks at me a little. "I know you," he says. "Eddy…"

"Eddy Johnson. I'm a book dealer."

"Figures," Wilkins says.

"Did you shoot that Pontiac?" Jones says.

"No."

"Who did?"

"I never seen the guy before."

"Why'd he shoot it?"

"I don't know. He didn't give a soliloquy beforehand."

"Maybe you'd like to explain that blood in the street."

"What blood?"

"Out in the street there."

"That's possum blood," Raoul says. "A possum got hit last night."

"Last night?"

"Yeah. They're nocturnal, you know."

"Possum blood, eh? Wilkins," he says, "go get a sample of it." He says to Raoul, "Maybe you'd like to come downtown and wait with us for the lab results."

"I didn't do anything."

"What about you?" Jones says to me. "You got anything else to add?"

"No."

"All right, I'm taking you in, Johnson. You're under arrest. You got the right to—"

"Yeah, yeah," I say.

"Tell him the truth," Raoul says to me.

I stare at him, but Raoul is looking at Jones.

"What truth, kid?" Jones says.

"*I* shot the gun."

"*You* shot that Pontiac?"

"It was an accident. I was playing around with the gun, and it went off."

"Is that right?" Jones asks me.

I shrug.

"He's my Big Brother," Raoul says. "I don't have a dad."

"You volunteer as a Big Brother?" Jones says.

"Sure."

"Don't they do background checks?"

"He's teaching me about rare books and stuff. His visits

mean a lot."

"Kid, something tells me you're as full of shit as he is."

"You don't have to talk to him like that," I say.

Jones says to me, "I still should take you in."

"Do what you want. But the boy's mother doesn't get home till eight. He'd be unsupervised until then, and if—"

"All right," Jones says. "Wilkins!"

Wilkins is on his knees in the street, scraping at the bloodied concrete with a shiny little instrument and tapping bits of it into a plastic ziplock bag. He looks up.

"Come uncuff this guy," Jones says. Wilkins stands and comes over. He uncuffs me. I rub my wrists.

"Thank you, officer," Raoul says.

"What about my gun?" I say.

"Don't push it," Jones says. "Come on," he tells Wilkins, "let's go."

They walk across the yard to their patrol car.

CHAPTER 19

WHEN THE COPS ARE GONE, I tell Raoul, "I thought for sure they would take me in."

"You're welcome."

"You're pretty quick on your feet, Raoul. You're okay."

He finishes his Dr. Pepper and says, "So, you have the rest of the money?"

"Yep. I'm ready to deal."

"I need to call Maria. Come on. There's a phone in the kitchen."

I follow him in the house. We walk through the living room into a country kitchen with lots of windows, worn-out linoleum, and a dinette set. There's a phone on the wall next to the back door.

Raoul tosses his empty soda can, opens the fridge, and gets a can of Mountain Dew.

"You want something?" he says.

"No. But listen. When I thought I might get arrested, I panicked a little and—"

"I'm keeping the hundred," Raoul says, pulling the tab on his soda.

"Yeah, sure. It's a deposit."

"What, then?"

"My business card."

"You want your business card back?"

"I don't have a lot left. I'm trying to put off printing more."

Raoul puts his soda on the table. He digs into his pocket, pulls out the card, and hands it to me. It's a little folded but not bad. I straighten it and put it in my wallet.

"Unbelievable," Raoul says.

"Hey, the minimum they'll print is like five hundred."

"Oh, I see."

"Just call Maria," I say.

He goes to the wall phone and dials a number.

I sit on one of the chairs and wait.

"I'm calling for Maria Juarez," he says. "This is her son."

He waits a little, then he says, "It's me. Everything's fine. Those guys showed up again, but it's okay, they're gone… I don't think we can stay here, though… Listen, there's a guy with me. A book dealer. Peggy Miller hired him to buy the stuff from us… Eddy Johnson. No, he's all right. He helped me get rid of those other dudes… He's looking to buy the stuff for the Millers… Okay."

He holds the phone out.

"She wants to talk to you."

I get up and take the phone, Raoul sits at the table.

"Hello?" I say.

A woman says, "Mr. Johnson? This is Maria Juarez. Raoul's mom."

"Hi. I'm the guy Peggy Miller hired to buy the book and photos."

"That bitch," Maria says.

"I just want to do the deal. I've been shot at twice since yesterday, and now your house is like ground zero. Raoul didn't tell you, but the guys who barged into your house last night were Capalettis."

"Oh my God."

"I know you want more than five hundred dollars and hate the Millers. I get it. But the sooner we do this deal, the better. So we can get out of the middle."

"I have to work till ten."

"That's six hours."

She thinks. Then she says, "You can come here. I'm at Casita Reynoso, a restaurant on Congress Avenue. Do you know it?"

Casita Reynoso… Just hearing the name of the place is jarring, like hearing the name of an ex-lover.

"Yeah, I know it."

"Bring Raoul to me. And bring five hundred dollars."

"The stuff is with you?"

"I've got it stashed nearby."

"Okay. We'll be there in fifteen minutes."

"You need to come in through the back. Raoul will show you. Let me talk to him."

"Okay." I hold the phone down and tell Raoul, "Your turn."

He takes the phone. He switches over to Spanish and I have no idea what they're talking about. Then he hangs up.

"Okay, let's go," he says.

CHAPTER 20

CASITA REYNOSO WAS MY FAVORITE breakfast spot. I'd go there weekday mornings about ten or ten-thirty. By then the early morning rush was done. The place would be deserted except for waitresses sitting at one of the tables counting tips. "Wherever you want, honey," one of them would tell me, and I'd slide into a booth in back. They'd bring me a mug of coffee and my usual: a plate of black beans, garlicky and smelling of cumin, with diced red and yellow bell peppers. On top would be two eggs over easy. I'd cut the eggs up, their yolks oozing out across the beans. I'd spoon some salsa verde on there... Oh, man!

And nobody would bother me. Now and then, without saying anything, one of the waitresses would come top off my coffee. When I was finished, I'd leave a tip on the table, take my ticket to the cash register to pay, and stroll out of there a better man.

But then the joint got discovered. Lobbyists and legislative aides from the state house, attorneys and real estate people, as well as some of the university crowd. Presumptuous people, snug and smug, talking loudly to each other about Vail and Palm Springs, famous golf courses and different cities' airports. Flourishing what Spanish they knew, they imagined they were making the waitress's day with their *gracias*, or covering the top of their coffee mug with a hand to prevent a refill: *no mas por favor.*

It became a real horror show.

My last time there—two years ago—I was one booth removed from a guy who was telling his buddy how spiritual his weekend fly fishing in Montana was (*it really got me back to me, you know?*). I was trying not to listen. Then a guy walked up to my booth and introduced himself as the new manager. He wanted to know if everything was okay. "Sure," I said, hoping that would end it. But no, he had a pot of coffee with him and was offering me a refill, beaming at me with this big beneficent smile, so freaking patronizing, as if being served like this by the manager was some incredible honor.

It was the last straw.

I waved him away, took my ticket to the register, and paid. I took one last look around, then walked out. I never went back.

CHAPTER 21

I'M DRIVING TOWARD DOWNTOWN. It's four-thirty, and I'm hurrying a little, hoping to beat the rush hour. On the other end of my truck's seat, Raoul talks nonstop. He hates school. He wishes he had a dog. He likes playing soccer. Can we stop for ice cream? His favorite flavor is mint chocolate chip. He's grown two inches in less than a year.

"How'd you get to be a book dealer?" he asks me.

"I just kind of fell into it. I always collected stuff, even as a kid."

"I've got a collectible," he says. "A *Famous Monsters* magazine. It's an anniversary edition."

"Oh yeah? What makes you think it's collectible?"

"It says so right on the cover."

"Uh-huh. That's what I thought. Forget it, Raoul. If everyone who buys it holds onto it, it'll never turn rare. It's a self-defeating prophecy."

"My mom got it for me for my birthday. The cover has Frankenstein choking Dracula."

"Good. It sounds neat. Enjoy it."

"It's a lot better than some stupid book about Texas."

"I'm not saying it isn't. But it'll never be worth half of what your mother paid for it. Sorry, that's just the way it works."

He doesn't like that, but he doesn't say anything.

By now we're southbound on Congress. Rush hour hasn't started yet. There are plenty of places to park in front of Casita Reynoso, but Raoul says, "We need to go around back. They're not open for dinner yet. Go to the light and take a left."

I do what he says, then turn north into the gravel alley behind buildings on the east side of Congress. It's uneven and dusty, with electric and phone lines crisscrossing overhead. The other side of the alley is brick walls and fences, some with razor wire.

"There," Raoul says, pointing to a small parking lot with some cars in it. I pull in and park. We get out of my truck, and I follow Raoul around a dumpster to an unmarked door. Next to the door is a wooden chair surrounded by hundreds of cigarette butts.

Raoul pulls the door open and we walk into the restaurant's kitchen. It's well-lit and clean, with red-tiled floors and white walls, stainless steel equipment and worktables, racks full of glasses and dishes. In one corner is a Hobart dishwasher like the one I spent summers working when I was in high school. In another corner, a guy sitting on a plastic milk crate is peeling potatoes. A huge bag of potatoes is next to him. He's letting the peels pile on the floor and, when he finishes a potato, he drops it into a pot of water.

"Hey, Raoul," he says, still peeling.

"What's up?"

"On the job, little man. You know."

It's like I'm backstage. On one of the stovetops I see a huge pot of black beans simmering. I can smell the cumin.

"Come on," Raoul says. I follow him toward a pair of swinging doors. We go through them into the public part of the restaurant.

The place is deserted except for two waitresses at a table toward the back. They're polishing silverware—sorting them into plastic racks they can pull from in a hurry when it's busy. They're in uniform. One of the waitresses is older. I remember her. She's tall and thin, her hair in a tight bun. The other waitress is young with long black hair. Raoul rushes to her, and she puts down what she's doing and hugs him. When she finishes squeezing him, she stands.

"Mr. Johnson?" she says.

I nod.

With her arm across Raoul's shoulders, she says, "Thanks for bringing my baby to me."

"I'm not your baby," Raoul says, shrugging off her arm.

"Boy, don't come in here disrespecting your mother like that," the other waitress says.

Maria and I shake hands. Her hand is small but firm and self-assured. "I'm Maria Juarez," she says.

"Call me Eddy."

"Let's go sit in a booth," she says. "Elena, can you watch Raoul?"

"I can watch him polish some of this silverware." She tells Raoul, "Come. Sit next to me."

He goes to her.

Maria leads me to a booth. It's like she's seating me as a customer, except when I slide into the booth, she sits across from me.

"You must think I'm not a very good person," she says.

"I'm not in the habit of judging."

"It was wrong of me to steal the book and photos. And I want you to know, that's the only time I ever stole from them. That's not who I am. It's just I got so mad when she fired me. How am I supposed to take a hit like that? I'm working three jobs, going to school…"

"Listen," I say. "You seem like a nice person. It makes sense to me what you did. On the other hand, if it's bothering you, you could just give the stuff back. I could deliver it to the Millers with your apologies."

Her eyes flash in anger.

"I'm not that sorry. Besides, it looks like Raoul and I are going to have to move."

"Yeah, that would probably be a good idea."

"You want something to drink? A cup of coffee?"

"No, I'm good. Let's just do this."

"You've got the money?"

I get my wallet out and pull some hundreds from it. "I already gave Raoul one hundred dollars," I say.

She turns around and calls to Raoul. "Did Mr. Johnson give you money?"

"He gave me one hundred dollars."

"Okay. Four hundred, then," she tells me.

I count four hundred-dollar bills, calling them out. Then I fold the hundreds and push them in my shirt's breast pocket. I look at Maria.

"Okay, I'll be right back with the stuff," she says.

She stands and goes through the swinging doors to the kitchen. I put my wallet away. Elena and Raoul are still polishing silverware without talking. I look up and see a painting on the wall over the booth—a Texas hill country watercolor: wildflowers in a sunny meadow, a weathered barn, some trees in the background. It's not bad.

Maria comes through the swinging doors carrying a brown paper bag folded flat. She comes to the booth and sits across from me, puts the bag on the table.

I unfold the bag. I look inside and see the Arnold.

I reach in my shirt pocket, get the four hundred dollars, and hand the bills to Maria. I reach in the bag and pull out the Arnold. It's small and heavy, bound in red calfskin with raised yellow lettering on its spine and cover. It's in mint condition. Lettering still fully colored, calfskin not too dry. It's beautiful.

I find some photos in the bag. Three of them. Polaroids full of pale pink flesh and a big white cowboy hat: Miller and some blond gal playing around on a rumpled bed. In one photo, Big Frank is on all fours and the woman is sitting on him, riding him like a horse. She's wearing the cowboy hat and nothing else. In another, Big Frank is wearing the hat. He's just lassoed her, it looks like, and is pulling her toward him. Boy howdy, as they say in Texas. There's no way the Millers want these going public, with or without a mayoral race to worry about. I spare myself looking at the third photo.

"Pretty wild," I say, shaking my head. I put the photos in the bag.

"There are things that, once you have seen them, can never be unseen," Maria says.

"You got that right."

"Raoul has seen them. I regret that as much as anything."

I open the Arnold and see the autograph. I flip to page 68 and look for the typo there: *bluebonnets* printed as *blusbonnets*. It checks out. I close the book.

"Okay," I say, putting the book in the bag, folding the bag shut. "I'll get this stuff to the Millers. After that, things should settle down, but it might take a while. I wouldn't go back to that house."

"You think those guys the mayor sent are with the Capalettis?"

"I know it for a fact. One of them was Franco Capaletti."

"I can't believe I put Raoul in danger. If anything had happened to him, I would never have forgiven myself."

"Well, luckily, nothing happened."

"Thanks for helping him and bringing him to me."

"He's a good kid. He's smart."

"A little too smart sometimes."

I look around the dining room—the long row of booths, the light coming in through the front door and windows. "You know, I used to come here for breakfast all the time."

"It's good food. I work the dinner."

"I didn't know they did dinner."

"They just started. They're trying to get a liquor license. You should come by sometime."

"Maybe I will." I stand, holding the bag. "Good luck, Maria." She stands too and we shake hands.

"Raoul," she says. "Say goodbye to Mr. Johnson."

Raoul looks over at me. "See you 'round, book man," he says.

CHAPTER 22

DRIVING THE HALF-DOZEN blocks to my room, I'm more relaxed than I've been all day. Or maybe it's just that I'm tired. It's been a tough twenty-four hours since I got sucked up into this mess. *The Case of the Purloined Arnold.* But things are looking up. I got the book I was hunting for. And I look to walk away with a tidy sum for all my trouble. I still have to worry about the Capalettis. I have a bump on my head, and the chili I ate at Joe Bob's won't quit churning. But I've learned over the years: you have to celebrate when you can. I can't think of any reason why, after stashing the Arnold, I shouldn't drift on over to the Dusty Jacket to toast my mixed fortunes.

It's five-thirty when I park across the street from the Alamo. I reach under my seat, get Franco Capaletti's gun, and put it in my holster. I grab the bag with the Arnold and get out of my truck.

Near the Alamo's entrance, there's a big sign that wasn't there this morning, nailed to two wooden posts sunk in the ground. It's painted white and says: *A public hearing regarding this property was held August 8th*. Almost two months ago. It goes into detail about the hearing in smaller writing I don't bother to read. Maybe they really are going to tear the place down. That's a whole other mess I'll have to deal with. If the Alamo is destroyed, I don't know where I'll go.

Inside, the lobby is deserted. Mrs. Nelson isn't at the counter, and the door behind it to her apartment is shut. I probably won't see her again until the first of next month.

I climb the stairs to the third floor, catch my breath, then head up the corridor. Halfway to my room, I stop and bang on the door to 313. James Palmer's door. It takes him a while, but he opens it wearing a bathrobe and slippers. He's unshaven and his eyes are out of focus. His hair is wild, like he's been in a wind tunnel.

"Eddy," he says. "What time is it?"

"A little after five-thirty."

"I must have fallen asleep."

"Listen," I say. "I need to park a book, but I don't want to leave it in my room. I'm worried some guys might come looking for it. I was thinking maybe I could leave it with you."

"Sure," he says. "Forty bucks."

"I was thinking twenty. It's just for a few hours."

He doesn't say anything. Then he holds out his hand. I give him twenty dollars and hand him the bag.

"I'll be back by nine, nine-thirty," I say.

"You got it, Eddy." He shuts the door. I hear him put the chain on.

I don't know what James's disability is. It doesn't seem to be physical, but it's serious enough that Social Security sends him a check each month. Some guys are just unlucky. They get dealt a bum gene, or somehow void their warranty for natural wear and tear. I find it's best not to ask.

I go along to my room and listen at the door a little before I unlock it. Holding Franco's gun, I open the door and go in. I check behind the door, then close and lock it and go look in the bathroom. The coast is clear.

I get the bourbon from the medicine chest, pour some, and carry the glass out into the main room. It's just the way I left it—the way that thug left it. Clothes tossed everywhere. Boxes of books dumped out. I put my glass on the table next to the chair, get on my knees, and make stacks of the books scattered on the floor. I push the stacks together into a little pile in the middle of the room. There's no damage to any of them, which is better than I expected. Just the Faulkner's dust jacket is ruined. It's still on the shredded mattress. Seeing it upsets me all over again.

I sit next to the pile of books and consider the clothes around me on the floor. I get up and drag them to the closet, shove them in, and close the door.

Sitting in the chair by the window, sipping the bourbon, I consider what my next move should be. I need to somehow get the photos to Big Frank Miller.

The book I need to return to Peggy Miller. Tonight, if possible. She and Robinson have already paid for it. By now, he's probably told her about my ruse with the Wodehouse. She doesn't believe it anymore, but I am a decent guy, or can be. I've never cheated a client or taken a book that doesn't belong to me.

When my glass is empty, I think about calling Peggy Miller. But the Dusty Jacket comes to mind also. For now, I just need to get out of this room.

CHAPTER 23

THE DUSTY JACKET is on 7th Street between Hackberry and San Jacinto—ten blocks from the Alamo. A little after six, I park across the street and go in.

Jack's behind the bar. Two guys are sitting on stools sharing a pitcher of beer. Otherwise the place is deserted. Jack doesn't have a happy hour or free hors d'oeuvres. He doesn't put out beer nuts. I climb onto the stool at the end of the bar, and Jack comes along and puts a bottle of Shiner Bock in front of me.

"And a shot of Johnnie Walker," I say.

He puts a shot glass next to my beer and pours some Johnnie Walker in it.

I shoot the whisky and motion for more.

"Tough day at the office?" Jack says, pouring another shot.

I shrug. "Same old, same old," I say.

"That's not what I heard. I heard you been using Franco Capaletti for target practice."

"That's just a misunderstanding."

"Someone should tell Luigi. He's got a price on your head."

"Says who?"

"It's all over town, Eddy. Fifteen hundred bucks."

"That's all?"

"Luigi's old school. He thinks everyone should just do him favors."

"Anyway, it's a misunderstanding. Like I said."

"I'm glad. But listen, in the meantime, I'd prefer it if you didn't come around. I don't need any trouble, Eddy."

"Okay, Jack."

He pours me another shot. "On the house. I hope everything works out."

He goes to the other end of the bar, starts wiping it with a towel.

I get down from my stool and go to the bathroom in back. I'm standing at one of the urinals when the bathroom door opens behind me. It's one of the guys sharing a pitcher. He's short and kind of pudgy, wearing a cheap suit. He steps up to the other urinal.

We're both doing our business, when he says without looking at me, "You're Eddy Johnson."

"Am I?" I say.

"Yeah, you're him."

"What if I am?"

"Don't worry, I ain't gonna take you out for no three grand."

I zip up and walk to the sink, wash my hands.

"Take care," I tell him before I leave.

"See you 'round," he says.

I walk to my stool and, standing next to it, toss back the shot Jack poured me. I drop three bucks on the bar and head for the door. As I go by Jack, I say, "It's up to three grand."

Looks like I'll be doing my drinking in my room. On my way there, I need to get something to eat. Maybe a pizza.

I'm at my truck, putting my key in the door, when two guys come up behind me. I can't see who they are. One of them puts a hand on my right arm above the elbow, with just enough pressure to keep me from doing anything stupid.

Oh hell, I think. I say, "Come on, guys. Don't do this."

The guy holding my arm laughs. "Don't worry, Mr. Johnson. We're with the Romanos."

"Yeah," the other guy says. "Joey wants to see you."

"Now?"

"Just get in the car."

He gestures toward a blue Lincoln Town Car pulling over to the curb behind my truck. Its windows are so dark I can't see inside. The driver—one of the guys I met at Joey's warehouse earlier—gets out, walks around, and opens a back door for me.

CHAPTER 24

THE TWO GUYS HUSTLE ME to the Lincoln's open door. When I get there, I see Joey inside the car, on the far end of the back seat. He gives me a little wave. I sit next to him. The driver shuts my door, goes around, and gets behind the wheel.

Joey's smiling, but it's a smile I'm not so sure about.

"Eddy," he says. "Long time no see."

He reaches to me. His hand falls on my thigh, just above the knee. I cringe a little, just a little, but Joey sees it.

"What's wrong, Eddy?" he says, taking his hand away. "You're not scared of me. Jeez, Eddy, you and me are friends."

"I'm sorry."

"Where to, boss?" the driver says.

"Just drive around."

The Lincoln starts moving, heading west on 7th.

"You don't have to be anywhere, do you, Eddy?"

"No."

"I keep hearing what a busy guy you are. I hear Eddy's done this and Eddy's done that. He's been here, he's been there."

I don't say anything.

Joey says, "I'm worried about you. You've got some big problems. I think you know how big. But when you came to see me this morning, you didn't even mention them. All you talked about was some little thing, strictly rinky-dink."

"But—"

"I'm a friend of yours, Eddy. And you held out on me. That makes me worry. I say to myself, *maybe Eddy's one of these guys who doesn't know who his friends are. Or maybe a guy who knows but keeps forgetting.* And I really hope that's not the case. Because, you know what happens sooner or later to a guy who doesn't know who his friends are?"

"What, Joey?"

"Happens every time. Ulcers. Rotten, lousy ulcers. You don't want any, believe me."

"But, Joey. I swear to God. When I went to see you, I had no idea what was going on."

The Lincoln turns right on Stetson. We head north.

"It was after I saw you that I found out who I shot last night. I didn't know the Capalettis were involved. I swear to God. I would have told you. I would have known to tell you."

"It's good to hear you say that, Eddy. The way some people been putting it, the way they make it out—well, you know how people are. Always ready to think the worst. But, no matter what they said, all I kept saying was, *I got to talk to Eddy. Let me talk to Eddy.*"

The Lincoln stops at a red light at 10th Street and signals a left.

"Everything happened so fast, Joey. It's a big crazy mix-up. I never meant to shoot anybody. The first time, last night, it was dark and—"

"You don't have to explain to me, Eddy."

"I value the friendship we have."

"I know you do. And I appreciate it. You've always been an easy guy to have around."

"If I've created a problem for you, I hope you'll give me the chance to make it up."

"That's music to my ears. Sounds so good…"

"I'll do anything."

Joey laughs. "Good old Eddy." He punches my left arm with a playful jab. Everything between my elbow and shoulder goes numb.

I laugh too.

While I'm rubbing my arm, Joey leans forward and tells the driver, "Okay, back to headquarters."

The Lincoln swings around and heads south.

"Relax," Joey says. "Everything's going to work out."

CHAPTER 25

IN FRONT OF the Romano Brothers warehouse, Joey and I get out of the Lincoln. It drives away. Outside the main entrance, Joey stops me on the sidewalk.

He says, "One thing. Before we go in."

"What, Joey?"

"I've got lots of tough guys working for me. Guys like Rollo. You know—real animals. The thing is, except for Rollo, they don't really know you. And they're kind of in awe of what you've done—going up against the Capalettis on your own."

"But those were accidents."

"Sure. You know that and I know that. All I'm saying is, there's no reason why my boys have to know."

"But—"

"I'm not saying brag about it. Just play it cool. Hey, a magician doesn't explain his tricks. So what if he gets a little applause?"

"Okay, Joey."

He opens the door and we go in the little waiting room. Nobody's there.

"Carol!" Joey shouts.

A door behind the receptionist's desk opens and a gorgeous blond comes in, voluptuous and saucy in tight black leather pants and a purple tank top. Her shoulders are deeply and wonderfully tanned.

"Heya, Mr. Romano," she says. "Sorry I wasn't at the desk. I had to pee."

"Any calls while I was out?"

"Yeah, a couple. Let me see... Guy called from Nevada Publications. DiBernardo. He said the truck should get here tomorrow afternoon."

"Did he say if he's sending the cookbooks?"

"He didn't mention them."

"Who else?"

"That guy from the Porn Palace. He says he can come up with two grand, maybe three by noon tomorrow, and the rest of what he owes by the—"

"Yeah, yeah," Joey says. "Hey, Carol. You know who this guy is?" He grabs my arm and pulls me close.

She looks at me. "Yeah. He was here this morning."

"I mean besides that."

"No."

"This is the guy who shot Franco Capaletti."

"Dead-Eye Eddy?" she says. "Wow." She looks me over. It's like she's seeing me for the first time. "You're the first guy I ever met who had a contract out on him."

"Hell," Joey says. "That don't mean nothing to Eddy."

"I guess not," she says.

"All right, thanks for staying late, Carol. I appreciate it. You can go now."

"Okay, Mr. Romano. No problem. It was an honor to meet you, Mr. Johnson."

"Likewise."

"Come on, Eddy," Joey says. "Let's go in my office."

He ushers me into his office and shuts the door.

He laughs and slaps me on the back. "See? What did I tell you?"

"Dead-Eye Eddy?"

"That's the first I heard that. I like it."

"But I don't want a reputation as a tough guy. A reputation like that is trouble. I've already got a price on my head."

"Eddy," Joey says.

The way he says it, I shut up.

"Sit down," he says.

I sit in a chair in front of his desk. I look at my watch. It's ten till seven.

Joey goes around behind the desk, grabs a bottle of Chivas, and pours into two glasses. He hands me a glass, then sits in his swivel chair.

"Salute," he says. We clink glasses, then both swallow some Chivas.

He puts his drink down. He says, "Now listen, Eddy. I'm not happy. You come see me this morning after shooting Franco Capaletti. Then you shoot him again. You make it look like I'm involved. All of a sudden—I don't even know why—I'm at war with the Capalettis. What the hell?"

"I'm sorry, Joey."

"You got me into this, and now you're gonna be a busy guy making sure I come out on top."

I nod.

"Now stop feeling sorry for yourself. So far, you've done okay. You're with me, which is about the only place you're safe from the Capalettis. And—let's face it—it's a miracle you tangled with Franco twice and didn't end up in the aquifer."

"I know."

"You're a lucky guy," Joey says. "Now tell me everything."

"Well, first off, the client I'm working for is Big Frank Miller."

"The guy running for mayor?"

I nod. "Actually, I'm working for his daughter. They had a book stolen. The Arnold I told you about. The thief offered to sell it back and they hired me to handle it. It seemed like a simple enough job. But then, whenever I got close to the Arnold, the Capalettis would show up and start shooting at me."

"To get the Arnold?"

"No. That's the thing. What I didn't know until this afternoon is that there were some photos tucked inside the Arnold when it was stolen. That's what the Capalettis want."

"I don't get it," Joey says.

"Dirty photographs of Big Frank Miller and some woman."

"Holy shit."

"I know, right?"

"So, what—the Capalettis get the photos and put the squeeze on Miller?"

"No. It turns out they're working for Mayor Travis."

"The Capalettis and the mayor in cahoots," Joey says. "Son of a bitch."

He's angry—exactly what I'm trying to avoid.

"Maybe just for this one thing," I say.

"No, I been suspecting something for a while. I haven't won a public-school textbook contract in like six months. Usually the school board spreads the wealth around, but not lately. That scumbag mayor. I ought to blow his house up."

Joey slams his fist on his desk. Then it's over. His anger is gone. He says, "Hey, if Luigi wants to use politicians, I can play that way. I've seen the polls. It looks to me like this Miller guy is practically a shoo-in."

"That's why the mayor wants the photos so bad."

Joey laughs. "Leave it to Luigi to pick the wrong candidate." He stops laughing.

"Eddy," he says. "I want this Miller guy. I want him in my pocket. You understand?"

"Sure."

"And you're the guy who's gonna get him for me. You've got to get those photographs."

"I've got them," I say. "The Arnold too. I got them stashed at the Alamo."

"My man." Joey reaches across his desk and we high five. He says, "The Alamo. I thought they tore that place down."

"I don't know why everyone thinks that."

He shrugs. "Anyway, great—we're in business. The photos are good and juicy?"

"Oh yeah. He's like this big hairy pink whale, and he's with this young gal—she's maybe half his age—and they're playing with lassoes, cowboy hats…"

"Guy likes to party," Joey says. "He must be going nuts, worrying about that stuff going public. You take him the Arnold and the photos with my compliments. Tell him I'm happy to help."

"Okay. The thing is, Joey, he doesn't know the stuff is missing. His daughter's the one who hired me. She never told him the Arnold was taken. And she doesn't know about the photos."

"Hmmm," Joey says. "That changes things. It might seem to him like we're leaning on him instead of doing him a favor…"

"I've got an idea about that. Since the daughter hired me to get the Arnold, I could go ahead and take it to her first. Then I can go to Big Frank Miller and give him the photos—tell him thanks to you his daughter never saw them."

"Good, I like it. Okay, that's what we'll do." He drinks some more Chivas, draining his glass. He grabs the bottle and pours us both some more. "You know what, Eddy?" he says, clinking glasses with me again. "This could turn out to be one of the best things that's ever happened to either one of us."

Somehow, I doubt it.

He says, "You get those photographs to Miller, it'll go a long way toward making us even."

"I appreciate it, Joey."

"Not totally even. I've still got this war with the Capalettis to deal with. And you're going to help me with that, too. My guys will feel a lot better knowing they have Dead-Eye Eddy on their side."

Dead *Guy* Eddy is probably more like it.

"All right," Joey says. "Let's get this done tonight. I'm gonna give you an escort. Someone to protect you. And now," he says, "before you go, I've got a surprise."

"What's that?"

"The guy you were asking about. The jerk with a scar on his face."

"You found him?"

CHAPTER 26

THEY FOUND HIM ALL RIGHT.

Joey leads me deep into the warehouse, far from the loading docks, the idle pallet jacks and sorting tables and fleets of picking carts. I follow him down long claustrophobic aisles of thirty-foot-tall skid rack.

At the end of one aisle we take a final turn and there he is—the lowlife thug who busted into my room last night. The poor bastard. He's slumped on a wooden chair, held by coils of thick rope. The way his head hangs forward, to one side, I doubt he's conscious. His face is puffy and bruised. Dried blood trails from his mouth. Someone has worked him over good.

Near him on another chair, reading a comic, is one of the guys I met in Joey's office this morning. When he sees me and Joey, he drops the comic and stands. "Heya, boss," he says. "Mr. Johnson."

"How's it going, Sal?" Joey says.

"He's alive, just like you said."

"Eddy, Sal here's the guy who brought him in."

"Way to go, Sal."

"Aw, it was nothing. I played a hunch he might be in a bar Rollo seen him in before—the Bookend, on Rio Grande. And he was there. Besides, it's an honor to do something for Dead-Eye Eddy."

I look at Joey, and he gives me a wink.

"Franco Capaletti's nemesis."

"His what?" Joey says.

"Nemesis," Sal says. "The thing that's got his number."

The thug in the chair—slumped against the rope—starts to stir. He groans.

"He's waking up," I say.

"Yeah, waking up," Sal says. "Had himself a little nap."

We watch him. His head is moving, but still hanging forward.

"Did you find out who he was working for?" Joey says.

"I knew I forgot something."

"It's okay. I already know," I say.

"All right, then," Joey says. He steps up to the guy, pokes him in the shoulder. "Yo. Rise and shine."

The guy lifts his head and looks at Joey. His eyes are dazed and confused.

"You jerk. You should never have played Mr. Tough Guy with my pal Eddy here."

The guy looks past Joey and sees me. We make eye contact. "Eddy," he says. "I'm sorry. Let me make it up to you."

"Sal," Joey says. Sal pulls a pistol from his holster. He gives it to Joey.

"No…" I hear the thug saying. "Please…"

Joey checks to see that the pistol's loaded. He cocks it.

"You're not going to kill him," I say.

"No. You are."

He holds the pistol out to me.

"I don't want to kill him, Joey."

"You're the one he screwed over."

He puts the pistol in my hand.

Sal says, "Do one of them fancy tricks of yours!"

"Eddy," I hear the guy in the chair saying.

"Joey," I say. I'm gesturing, pleading with him, and the gun in my hand goes off.

Joey and I stare at each other.

Sal says, "What a shot!"

No, I think. I turn and look at the guy in the chair. I see the bullet hole in his forehead. Right between the eyes. Blood is draining out of it.

"And you weren't looking or anything!" Sal says.

"Not bad, Eddy," Joey says. "You know? I think maybe you got something going."

I stand holding the pistol, staring at the dead guy. The only guy I ever killed. I don't even know his name.

CHAPTER 27

I LEAVE THE ROMANO BROTHERS warehouse at eight-thirty, in the same blue Lincoln that brought me there. I'm in the back seat, next to a guy named Sonny. Sonny's big and serious. He stares straight ahead, giving off an air of menace that scares me even though he's my escort. His body strains and stretches his dark suit, and he's holding an Uzi. In his big meaty hands, it looks like a toy.

We're going to the Alamo to get the Arnold and the photos. We're about halfway there when the driver says, over his shoulder, "It sure is an honor driving you, Dead-Eye."

"Thanks," I say.

"I heard how you plugged that guy—right between the eyes—without even looking."

"Shut up, Tony," Sonny says. It's the first thing he's said since we got in the car. Nobody talks after that until we get to the Alamo. Tony pulls over to the curb and stops.

"You ready?" Sonny says. I nod.

"Okay, let's go," he says.

We get out of the car. We go up the steps to the Alamo's

front door and go in the lobby. Nobody's around. We head up the stairs.

When we get to the third floor, we walk down the hall to my room, still without seeing anyone. I unlock my door and stand aside to let Sonny in. I wait in the doorway, watching up and down the corridor while, inside my room, Sonny turns the light on and walks around checking things out. He looks in the closet, in the bathroom.

"Okay," he says when he's satisfied. I come in, shut the door, and lock it.

"Where's the stuff?" Sonny says.

"I got it stashed with a guy across the hall."

"Well, let's go get it." He unlocks the door.

"Just wait here," I say.

"I don't think so."

"All right, Sonny. But hang back, okay? Let me talk to him. You'll just scare him."

Sonny follows me into the corridor. He waits behind me holding his Uzi while I knock on James Palmer's door. James opens it a little—it's still on its chain—and sees it's me.

"Hey, Eddy," he says. "You want your stuff back?"

"Yes."

"Hold on," he says. He shuts the door, then opens it again, still on its chain. He slides the folded bag through the opening.

"Thanks, James."

"You bet, Eddy. Hey, did you see that sign in front about the public hearing? What does it mean? Are they going to kick us out, do you think?"

"I don't know."

"But where am I supposed to go? I can't afford anyplace else." He sees Sonny then and slams his door shut. I hear him slide the deadbolt.

Sonny and I go back to my room. I shut and lock the door.

"Let me see the photos," Sonny says.

I go to the desk, open the bag, and pull the Arnold out. It really is gorgeous. I get the three Polaroids from the bag and hand them to Sonny.

He sits on the bed. He puts the Uzi down, then puts on some reading glasses. He holds the photos up so he can see them. He shows no reaction, which is saying something. He puts the reading glasses away.

"Okay," he says. "We call Joey."

I hand him the phone.

I'm standing, watching him dial, when he says, "Do me a favor, will you? Stay away from the window."

I realize I'm right in front of it. I back away, then go sit at the desk.

Sonny says into the phone, "This is Sonny. Put Joey on." He waits, then he says, "Yeah, we got the stuff. No problem... I don't know. He's right here, you want to talk to him?"

He motions for me to come over, I stand and go get the phone receiver from him. "Hello?" I say.

"Eddy," Joey says.

"Yeah, Joey."

"That's great you got the stuff. Now you got to deliver it. I poked around a little and the daughter should be home. Her old man is holed up at the Fiscal Hotel. He keeps a suite of rooms there. The Longhorn Suite, on the eighteenth floor."

"Okay, Joey."

"You tell Miller the photos are a gift. A token of my esteem."

"Yeah, like we talked about."

"I don't want to make this guy nervous. Don't mess it up."

"I won't."

"Let me talk to Sonny."

I hand the receiver to Sonny and go sit at the desk.

Sonny listens to Joey for what seems like a long time. Now and then he says *okay* or *yeah* or *gotcha, boss.* Then he hangs up.

He puts the Polaroids in one of his jacket pockets. "All right, let's go," he says. He stands and picks up the Uzi. I put the Arnold in the paper bag and fold it shut.

Someone knocks on my door.

Sonny and I freeze. We wait, listening. There are some more knocks.

Sonny motions for me to say something.

"Who is it?" I say.

"Telegram for Eddy Johnson," a guy's voice says.

"Slip it under the door."

"Sorry, Mr. Johnson, you have to sign for it."

I look at Sonny. He motions for me to come closer. I do, and he whispers in my ear, "Go see if the car is still there."

I go to the window and look out. The Lincoln is there. I give Sonny a thumbs up.

"Mr. Johnson?" the guy outside the door says.

"Just a minute," I say.

Sonny motions me over toward the bathroom, well out of the way. He goes to the door. He swings the Uzi up and—shooting from the hip with both hands—he sprays the door for maybe three seconds.

When he stops shooting, my ears are ringing from the noise. My room is thick with the smell of exploded gunpowder. I have no idea how many bullets he fired. Enough that chunks of the door are missing.

Sonny turns the doorknob so it unlocks. He pulls the door open and looks in the hall.

"Come on," he says. "Let's go."

I follow him through the open door. We step over a guy sprawled across the carpet in front of my room, red blood soaking through his shirtfront, his pistol next to him. It's the guy I talked to in the bathroom at the Dusty Jacket. The price on my head must have gone up again. But there's no time to worry about that. I keep up with Sonny, flying down the stairs two, three at a time—stairs I usually trudge up and down.

When we get to the lobby, there's another guy from Hoods-R-Us, gun in hand. But we're moving so fast he only gets one shot off—a bullet hits the wall behind us—before Sonny slams into him like a freight train, knocking him backward through the glass of the front door. The guy lands on his back outside, on top of the steps. Sonny sprays him with the Uzi until he's a bloody mess.

We duck through what's left of the door, and hurry around the dead guy and down the steps to the sidewalk.

Sonny yanks open a back door of the Lincoln, jumps inside, scoots over, and I jump in.

I'm still pulling the door closed as the Lincoln jerks away from the curb. We pick up speed fast, doing fifty when we hang a right on Rio Grande, sliding through the turn. Then we slide through another turn, onto 10ᵗʰ Street.

Tony's doing at least sixty when we go through a red light. We force a pickup truck onto the sidewalk and into a lamppost. We bounce over the crest of a hill and head toward Lamar.

A few blocks later, Tony slows the Lincoln to normal speed. He turns right onto an unlit residential street. He drives north a couple blocks, takes a left, then a right. He's cruising, keeping an eye on the rearview mirror. He says, "What the hell happened back there? Was it the Capalettis?"

"Naw, couple a jerks," Sonny says. "Did we get away clean?"

"Looks like it."

Two guys are gunned down where I live, one of them through the door of my room—from the inside—and I'm getting away clean? But I guess it's not me they're talking about.

"Where now?" Tony says.

"The west side," I say. "Big Frank Miller's house."

I sit forward, holding onto the back of the front seat, and give him directions.

CHAPTER 28

IT'S TEN O'CLOCK WHEN WE get to the Millers' place. Tony pulls up to the gate. He cuts the Lincoln's lights.

"I have to call up to the house," I say. I open my door and get out, walk to the little box near the gate. I push its button a few times.

"Yes?" a woman's voice says. It's Peggy Miller.

"Miss Miller, this is Eddy Johnson."

She doesn't say anything.

"Miss Miller?"

"Mr. Johnson, leave me alone. Do you want me to call the police?"

"I've got the Arnold."

She doesn't say anything.

"Miss Miller?"

"I don't believe you."

"I found Maria and bought it from her."

"Isn't that what you told Bart Robinson? This makes the third time you've claimed to have the book."

"But I really do have it this time."

"I don't trust you."

"Come on. I just want to get the book to you and be square. I've already been paid." I listen a while, then add, "I'm sorry for the way I treated Mr. Robinson."

"You pulled a gun on him!"

I'm so focused on talking into the box, listening to Peggy Miller, I don't notice Sonny. He's standing next to me.

"What's the hang-up?" he says.

"She's nervous."

"Hey, lady," Sonny says into the box. "Open the gate."

She says, "Who is speaking, please? Mr. Johnson, who is this person?"

"He's like my bodyguard."

"Well, he needs to learn some manners."

"We just want to give you the stupid book," Sonny says.

There's no answer. I motion for Sonny to keep quiet. I tell her, "I don't have time for this. If you want the book, open the gate. You got one minute."

Sonny and I step away from the box.

"I can bust this gate open," he says. "No problem."

"No, that's not a good idea," I say.

I hear a buzz. The gate starts sliding open. Sonny and I get in the Lincoln and Tony drives up the driveway. He still has the lights off.

We stop in front of the house, Sonny and I get out. I'm holding the Arnold. I've got it out of the paper bag so she can see it. We walk up the steps to the big mahogany door. I reach for the brass spaniel's head, to bang it, but the door opens first.

It opens just a little, on a chain. Peggy Miller is peering out. She sees Sonny, and she's drawing back, about to shut the door, when she sees the Arnold.

"Daddy's book," she says.

I hold it up so she can see it better.

"Give it to me," she says.

I hand it to her through the door. She leaves the door open as she handles the book clumsily. She turns it this way and that, looks at the front cover a while, then opens the book and finds the autograph.

"This is it, all right," she says. "Oh, I'm so relieved. I'm sorry I doubted you, Mr. Johnson."

"I don't care about that. I'm just glad it's back where it belongs."

"You're welcome," Sonny says.

She gives him a look but doesn't say anything.

"Thank you, Mr. Johnson. Now please go. And don't ever contact me again."

"Sure," I say. "I'll wait for *you* to call."

She shuts the door.

CHAPTER 29

THE FISCAL HOTEL IS A SWANKY JOINT downtown on 6th Street, an historical hotel reeking with tradition. Its old lobby is cavernous and still, oak paneled with occasional dim lighting. There's potted ferns and leather chairs and oil paintings of longhorn cattle and oil rigs.

Sonny and I walk through all the atmosphere to the elevators. One of them is open. We go in. I push the button for the eighteenth floor, the doors close, we start going up. Sonny pulls pieces of his Uzi from under his jacket, snapping them together. He assembles the gun easily and quickly.

We stop going up and the elevator doors open, we step out into an elegant corridor. A brass plaque on the wall says the Longhorn Suite is to the right. I lead Sonny that way.

When we get to the suite's entrance, I knock on the door. We wait, but nothing happens.

I knock some more.

"Yes?" a man's voice says from behind the door. "Who is it? What do you want?"

"I need to see Big Frank," I say.

"Big Frank's not here."

"I really need to see him."

Sonny motions for me to get out of the way. He's stepping back from the door.

"Come on, it's important," I say to the guy behind the door.

"Leave a message at the desk downstairs."

Sonny hurls himself, shoulder first, against the door. It gives way with a splintering crash. The door hardly slows him down. He goes through it, on into the suite, disappearing among flying bits of wood and hardware.

Well, okay then. I go in after him. I step over the rubble, including the guy I was talking to. He's unconscious, sprawled on the floor on his back. He's an older guy, wealthy-looking, dressed in a fancy suit.

Just ahead of me, Sonny's in a fancy living room, pointing his Uzi at a couple guys in armchairs.

They're guys like the one that got flattened—prosperous, mid-fifties, wearing business suits. They've got their jackets off. On a table between them there's a bottle of bourbon and three glasses. One of the men is smoking a cigar. He decides to talk to me instead of Sonny.

"Just what in the hell do you mean, busting in here like this?" he says.

"Sorry about the door," I say. "And your buddy. I need to see Big Frank."

"You'll clear on out of here if you know what's good for you," the guy with the cigar says. "And tell your friend to put that gun away."

"Don't worry about him. Where's Big Frank?"

"Hell if I know. Big Frank lets us use the suite when he's not around. Sometimes he shows up, sometimes he doesn't, end of story."

"Okay, I guess we try Plan B," I say. "Sonny?"

"Which one?"

I point to the other guy.

"Hey, wait a minute," the other guy says. He's talking to me but watching Sonny. "What's Plan B?"

"Sonny finds out where Big Frank is."

"Don't let them scare you, Cooper," the guy with the cigar says.

Sonny walks over to Cooper and stands next to him.

Cooper says, "Hey, let's not rush into anything."

I gesture for Sonny to hold up. I tell Cooper, "All right, last chance. Where's Big Frank?"

"Cooper," the guy with the cigar says.

"I don't know where he is," Cooper says. "I swear to God."

"Oh yeah? Then why's your pal so worried?"

"All right all right, he's in there." He points to a door on the far wall.

"Damn you, Cooper," the guy with the cigar says.

I say, "Sonny, get rid of these guys. The guy in the doorway too. Don't hurt them. Just get them out of here."

"Okay."

"And tell them to keep their mouths shut."

Sonny nods.

I pull my pistol out and walk to the door Big Frank Miller is supposedly behind.

CHAPTER 30

I OPEN THE DOOR and step into a bedroom. The bed is a king-sized four-poster with a white lace canopy.

Big Frank's on the bed naked, on his hands and knees. A beautiful young woman—also naked—is sitting on his back. She's riding him like he's a horse, hanging on the best she can while he bounces around on the mattress.

Neither of them notice me.

Big Frank slows down—the old guy is getting tired—and the woman reaches around and slaps him on the butt. She says, "Get a move on, darlin. We've got lots of trail to ride before the sun goes down." Big Frank neighs and, with a tossing of his head, starts bouncing around like crazy.

I say, "Big Frank. Excuse me."

The woman sees me. She sees the gun in my hand, and it scares her. In a flash, she's off Big Frank, rolled across the mattress and out of sight behind the bed.

I quickly put the gun away.

"What the hell?" Big Frank says. He looks around and sees

me. "You," he says.

I say, "I'm sorry. I need to talk to you."

The woman scrambles up off the floor and into the bathroom and shuts its door. I hear it lock.

"Damnit," Big Frank says. "Look what you went and did." He stands, grabs a red bathrobe that's draped across a chair. He pulls the bathrobe on and ties its sash.

"What's your name again?" he says.

"Eddy Johnson."

He walks over to me. "Listen, Eddy. Do me a favor. Don't ever interrupt me when I'm with a woman."

"Yes sir."

"I don't think that's too much to ask."

"No, you're right. I'm sorry."

"You rascal." Big Frank walks to an armchair and sits. He gets a half-smoked cigar from an ashtray on a little table by the chair and puffs it to life. He looks at me through rising smoke.

He says, "You're not any client of that rehabilitation place my daughter works at, are you?"

"No sir, I'm not."

"Then why were you at my house last night?"

"Your daughter hired me. I'm a book dealer."

"Peg?" Big Frank says. "Hell, all she ever reads is *TV Guide*."

Behind me the bathroom door opens. The woman comes out. She's dressed now, in a fancy gown and heels. Her hair is all fixed up. What a doll!

Big Frank says, "Jenny. How come you're dressed?"

"I'm taking off," she says.

"But we just got started."

"Sorry, sugar."

"Hell, this guy's leaving."

She blows him a kiss. "Call Danny," she says. "We'll do it again sometime."

She turns and walks through the open door to the living room. Where Sonny is.

"Excuse me," I tell Big Frank and I go after her. I find her standing frozen in the middle of the living room. Sonny, sitting in one of the armchairs, has her covered with the Uzi. Cooper and his buddy—the guy with the cigar—are gone.

"Sonny," I say. "It's okay. Let her go."

He lowers the Uzi.

She walks to the entranceway. The guy that was lying there is gone now too. She stumbles a little getting through the rubble, then she's gone.

"What's the deal?" Sonny says. "Is he in there?"

"Yeah."

"Well, let's give him the photos and scram."

"Give them to me," I say. I step toward him, holding out my hand.

"Joey wants *me* to give them to Miller."

"You don't even know him."

"It's what Joey wants."

I say, "Okay. But let me do the talking."

CHAPTER 31

WE GO IN THE BEDROOM. Big Frank is still in the armchair, puffing on his cigar. He says to me, "What's going on around here?" He points to Sonny and says, "Who the hell is this?"

"He's like my bodyguard."

"What happened to Cooper and them?"

"They're all right. They left."

"Well?" he says. "You've gone to all this trouble. What do you want?"

I say, "Yesterday, your daughter came to see me. She wanted me to get a book of yours that was stolen from your house."

"A book of mine? Peg never said anything about it."

"She didn't want you to worry."

"What book is it?"

"*Dear Sweet Texas.*"

"My Arnold!"

"It's okay, nothing happened to it. I got it back. I took it to your daughter just before we came here."

Big Frank smiles. "It's autographed, you know."

"Yes. It's beautiful."

"Good old Arnold. He always was one of my favorites."
He recites:

One lone thought my poor brain vexes.
Why did God make just one Texas?
Why didn't He make two or three?
Why not Texas sea to sea?
Why not Texas all around the planet?
Why not, Lord? Why not, damnit?

"Yessir," Big Frank says. "That Arnold sure could write."

"Good stuff," I say.

"Verses 232 and 233. I had to memorize them in high school. Known 'em ever since."

Big Frank thinks of something. "Wait a minute. Weren't there some… You didn't notice if there were any…"

"Photographs?" I say.

"Damn. Where are they? My daughter hasn't seen them, has she?"

"No sir. She never knew about them. I took the Arnold to her, like I said. But I thought I should bring the photographs to you."

"You've got them?" he says. "Let me see."

"Yes sir. But first, there's something I need to tell you. About how I got the photographs."

"What's that?"

"The reason I need Sonny here for protection is because some other people are looking for the photographs too, and they'll do anything to get them. They've already tried to kill me twice."

"What people?"

"The Capalettis. See, what happened—Mayor Travis found out about the photographs. He hired the Capalettis to get them. He wants to make them public."

"That pointy-headed son of a bitch."

"The thing is, because of the Capalettis, I couldn't get the photographs on my own. I needed help. So I went to a friend of mine. An influential member of the business community.

"When he heard the book was stolen from you, and that the photographs could hurt your campaign, he got upset. He made it a personal priority to get the stuff returned to you. You have him to thank—not me."

"Who are we talking about?"

"Joseph Romano."

"You mean *Joey* Romano? That yankee-ass Italian... I can tell you right now: there's no way he's getting his filthy hands on me."

"It's not like that," I say. "Mr. Romano just likes your politics. The photographs are his gift to you."

"No strings attached?"

"Only that you win."

Sonny clears his throat. He says, "Actually, Mr. Miller, there is one thing Joey wanted me to mention."

"Here we go," Big Frank says.

"What are you talking about?" I say to Sonny.

He ignores me. He says to Big Frank, "Joey says don't worry—blackmail ain't his style. But he says to remind you that if you're mayor, you'll be reviewing bids for the book concession out at the airport. Joey would like it if his bid wins."

"Hell, is that all?" Big Frank says.

"Joey says like a finder's fee."

"No problem," Big Frank says. "You tell him he's a reasonable man. If his bid is in any way defensible, I'll pick it."

"I'll tell him," Sonny says.

He steps toward Big Frank. "Here's the photographs," he says. He pulls them out of his jacket pocket and hands them over.

CHAPTER 32

BIG FRANK LOOKS AT THE TOP PHOTOGRAPH and smiles. "That gal sure was something." He flips through the photographs. "I don't know how you boys got these, but I sure am—"

He stops talking, flips through the photographs again. He says, "One's missing."

"What do you mean?" I say.

"Damnit now, don't play games with me. Where's the other one?" He says to Sonny, "So, blackmail ain't Joey Romano's style, eh?"

"Eddy?" Sonny says.

"There's three photographs."

"There's four," Big Frank says. "Joey Romano held one back."

"I was with him when he got them and there were only three."

"Then where's the other one?"

"I don't know."

"So, basically, the way things stand, that photo can go public anytime."

"Joey's got nothing to do with this," Sonny says.

"Yeah? Well, it looks like he's not going to have anything to do with the book concession out at the airport either."

"I'm sorry about this," I say.

"It makes me madder than a cow with its head stuck in a fence." Big Frank drops the photos on the bed, then goes to the window. He pulls back the curtain and stands looking out, watching traffic below on 6th Street.

Sonny nudges me. He whispers, "Joey's not going to like this."

"I don't like it either," I say.

"You know something?" Big Frank says, still looking out the window. "People don't think about what it's like to be a politician. They see the gravy—the bribes and kickbacks, the insider information. And sure, that's all there. You need to have incentives or people wouldn't run for office. But it is absolute hell being in the public eye." He comes back from the window. He says, "Boys, come with me. I want to show you something."

We follow him into the living room.

He goes to what looks like another bedroom, opens its door, and ushers us in.

Instead of a bed, the room is taken up by downtown Austin—a big scale model waist-high on a table. It reminds me of my Uncle Joe's model railroad setup: the village with its station, the mountain tunnel. But this is the city I live in. I see the river and its bridges. On the south side there's Barton Springs, the round convention center, even the pagodas of the Zen gardens in Zilker Park. On Congress Avenue, leading up to the capitol with its shiny dome, all the buildings are there. The detail is amazing: cars on roads, tiny people walking on sidewalks.

But something is different. West of Congress, there's an

unexpected cluster of tall gleaming towers, six or seven of them, joined above ground by enclosed walkways. They're set in a landscape of courtyard greenspaces, multi-tiered parking garages, Olympic pools under glass domes. It's as if an ultramodern space station has landed downtown.

"This is my baby," Big Frank says, pointing to the new buildings. "Santa Anna Towers. Ain't she something?"

Sonny says, "Are they residential?"

"Yessir. Downtown condos. They'll fetch a million dollars each someday."

I don't see the Alamo. I look for it, counting blocks up from the river, over from Congress, and I realize: one of Big Frank's towers is right where the Alamo should be.

"What about the Alamo Boardinghouse?" I say.

"The Alamo? That place is history. We're scheduled to knock it down in a couple months."

"Just as well," Sonny says.

"This is why I got into politics. The only sure way to get the go-ahead from the city was to get elected mayor. And I've about got that done. I've spent half a million dollars on my campaign, I'm well ahead in the polls... But now these dadgum photographs get loose. How the hell did that even happen?"

"One of the servants your daughter fired stole them."

"Oh. Was it that pantry gal?"

I nod.

"Yeah, I can see that. I can't really blame her... Shit. The hell of it is, Peg fired those servants because consultants said it was wrong to have so many. Bad for my image, they said. But look how that's turned out. Damned if I do, damned if I don't."

"I am so sorry," I say. "I thought these were all the photos. And I guarantee—like I said—Joey Romano is in no way responsible. He's gonna be as upset about this as you are."

"You got that right," Sonny says.

"Well, I can't just wait for that photo to surface. It's a straggler. I need to get it back with the herd."

I nod.

"And you're the fella that's gonna round it up."

"Me?" I say.

"Sure. You're fresh from the trail. Just backtrack a little. You'll find it."

"But I don't—"

"You get me that photograph, Eddy, I'll give you ten thousand dollars. In fact..." He reaches in a pocket of his bathrobe and pulls out a roll of money. It's rolled up tight, a rubber band around it. He hands it to me.

"That's five thousand. You bring me the missing photo, I'll give you another five."

I put the money in my pocket.

Big Frank tells Sonny, "You help Eddy do this, I'll give *you* two thousand. And Joey Romano can have the airport book deal."

Sonny nods.

Big Frank laughs. "Well, hell, boys. Welcome to the campaign."

We walk out into the living room.

"We'll get right on it," I say.

"Good."

"It was nice to meet you, Mr. Miller," Sonny says. "And rest assured, me and all of Joey's guys will be casting our ballots on your behalf."

"Glad to hear it. Now, if you fellas don't mind, I'm gonna take a shower and get dressed." He goes in the bedroom. As he's shutting the door, he says, "You all be careful, now."

CHAPTER 33

WE LEAVE THE SUITE, Sonny first. He hesitates at the entrance, leaning forward through the empty doorway and looking both ways. Satisfied, he steps out into the corridor. He gestures for me to follow.

I'm coming, making my way through the rubble, when the shooting starts. There's a pistol shot, then the roar of Sonny's Uzi. Through the doorway, I see him crouched in profile, spraying everything ahead of him.

By the time I get my pistol out, it's over.

"Come on!" Sonny shouts. He takes off running in the direction he was shooting.

I go through the doorway and chase him.

There's a big mess about three doors down that I have to hurdle. A tipped-over room service cart—the meal it was carrying scattered on the carpet among broken dishes. I see a T-bone steak, a baked potato. Also, face down, the guy who was pushing the cart. He's wearing a waiter's uniform. Near him is a pistol smeared with bleu cheese dressing.

I keep up with Sonny the best I can. He's really moving. He gets to a door marked STAIRS and goes through it. I go into the stairwell too, in time to see him making a turn on the landing below.

"Wait!" I shout, but he doesn't stop. I chase him down the stairs. I get to the fourteenth floor, I'm just keeping up, I say, "Sonny, stop! They'll be waiting at the bottom."

On the landing between the twelfth and thirteenth floors, he finally stops. I stand next to him catching my breath.

"We need to take the elevator," I say. "We have to look normal. Put your gun away."

"But what if there's cops?"

"Just act natural."

"I don't know. If there's cops, it might be better if we shoot our way out."

"No," I say. I try to sound firm. "No shooting. Put your gun away. If we play it cool, we can walk out of here, no problem."

"If some cop starts asking me a bunch of questions…"

"Don't sweat it."

"I got this thing about cops. When I'm talking to a cop, I get so crazy, I don't know what I'll do."

But he's breaking down the Uzi as he talks, putting pieces of it under his jacket.

"Okay," he says when the gun is hidden.

I say, "Relax. A cop starts talking to you, no problem. You make something up. They want to know why you're in the hotel, you were spending some time with a lady friend. What's her name? You can't tell because she's married. You see what I'm saying?"

"I don't know," Sonny says.

"If we get stopped, let me do the talking."

We walk down to the next landing, to a door with a big 12 stenciled on it.

"Just take it easy," I say.

I open the door and step out into a corridor identical to the one on the eighteenth floor. Of course, there's no dead guy sprawled on the carpet.

CHAPTER 34

SONNY AND I WALK TO where the elevators are. I push the *down* button, one of them opens with a ding. It's empty. We go inside, I push the button for the lobby, the doors slide shut. We go down.

"Cops," I say. "They're just people."

"My old man got killed by cops. My kid brother too. My uncle Sal, my cousin Anthony... But there ain't never been a Cigalese who, when he bought it, didn't take at least one cop with him."

"Sonny, you're thinking about this all wrong."

The elevator stops.

"Be cool," I say. The doors slide open and we're facing the lobby. We step out of the elevator and head for the 6th Street entrance. There's no sign of trouble—just the usual kind of crowd milling around. I don't see any cops.

We're about halfway across the lobby, when a guy I didn't notice before comes walking toward us. He's in his forties, tense, wearing a cheap wrinkled suit and dumb black shoes. A detective, no doubt about it—one I don't know.

He steps in front of us, holding his badge out so we can see it. "Excuse me, gentlemen," he says. "You wouldn't mind answering a few questions before you leave, would you? There's been a minor disturbance in the hotel this evening."

He's looking at Sonny, studying his face.

"We didn't notice anything," I say.

"What floor were you on?"

"The twelfth."

He's still looking at Sonny.

I say, "What happened, officer? I hope nobody was injured."

The detective says to Sonny, "Don't I know you?"

Sonny shrugs.

"You're Sonny 'the meatball' Cigalese. Aren't you?"

Sonny says, "I ain't no meatball."

I say, "This is my friend Billy Ray Jackson. He's visiting from Lubbock."

"Oh, I see. Gee, I'm sorry. My mistake."

"No harm done. Now, if we can be on our way…"

The detective says to me, "You know, its uncanny the resemblance your friend Mr. Jackson here bears to this Cigalese fella. He's a local thug we sometimes have to deal with. You've probably never heard of him."

"No, I haven't."

"His nickname is the meatball."

Sonny starts to tremble. I say, "That's very interesting, officer, but—"

The detective steps closer to Sonny. He says, right in his face, "Maybe you're curious to know, Mr. Jackson, why it is we call him the meatball."

Sonny doesn't say anything. He's shaking.

"It's because he's so stupid it's like he's got a meatball for a brain."

"All right!" Sonny shouts. He yanks a pistol and shoots it twice, both times into the detective's chest.

As the detective crumples to the lobby floor, someone yells, "Freeze, scumbag!"

I look and see a uniformed cop near the front desk. He must have just showed up. He's got his pistol leveled at us. Sonny and the cop start shooting at each other. I throw myself to the carpet. The dead face of the detective is right in front of me. I hear more shooting, then the thud of Sonny falling next to me, like a tree being felled. The way he lands and doesn't move again, I know he's dead.

I turn my head and look where the uniformed cop was. He's flat on his back on the carpet. He's not moving either.

I look around, everyone else in the lobby is hiding—lying flat on the carpet like me, crouched behind potted plants or ornamental columns. There aren't any other cops. I get to my feet, step from between the bodies of Sonny and the detective, and walk quickly toward the 6th Street entrance. Behind me, I hear the first murmurings of people who have witnessed something big.

I go through the door, out onto the sidewalk. It's late—after midnight. I don't see the Lincoln. Tony's around somewhere. He's probably cruising the block, passing the hotel every so often watching for us. But I can't hang around waiting.

I decide to walk to my truck. It's still parked in front of the Dusty Jacket on 7th Street, about five blocks away. I walk fast, trying to not seem panicked. My heart is pounding. Poor Sonny.

I need to call Joey, let him know what happened. Not only the shootout and Sonny getting killed, but the missing photo too. Giving bad news to Joey is something I don't look forward to. But I know I can't put it off.

CHAPTER 35

I TURN THE CORNER ONTO 7ᵗʰ Street and see my truck three blocks ahead, across from the Dusty Jacket.

This late at night, the street is deserted. The front door of the Jacket is propped open. The yellow light spilling from its doorway and front window is the only sign of life around. Probably the usual handful of late-night regulars are inside, lined up on their stools. I wouldn't mind joining them, but I promised Jack I'd stay away.

I hear sirens from all directions coming fast, converging on the Fiscal Hotel. I don't know where I should go—not back to my room, that's for sure—but I need to get off the street.

I reach my truck. I unlock it and get in. I turn the key and the engine turns over but doesn't start. I try again. Sparks and smoke come from the dash. Somebody rigged my truck! It's gonna blow! I open the door to get out and KABOOM! I'm flying through the air. I land on my back in the street. The door I was opening lands near me, its window shattered. I lift my head and look back at my truck, it's upside down, engulfed in flames. My ears are ringing from the explosion. I'm dazed, but I don't seem to be hurt. I manage to sit up.

Jack and his regulars come running out of the Dusty Jacket.

"Holy shit!" one of them says. "That's Eddy Johnson's truck!"

"What's left of it."

"Eddy!" Jack says. "Are you all right?"

He's on one knee next to me in the street, looking at me.

"I think so," I say. I try to get up, but Jack stops me.

Other people come up behind him. They're staring at me.

"It's him," someone says.

"There's not a scratch on him!"

"Gonna have to call Triple A, Eddy!"

"Amazing!"

I'm still sitting. Jack is methodically touching different parts of me—my legs, arms, shoulders—looking for damage.

"I don't see where anything's wrong," he says. "You must be the luckiest guy in the world."

"Lucky…" I say.

"Let's get you up. Get you out of the road."

He goes behind me, slides an arm through each of my armpits, and lifts me to my feet. He stands close to me, an arm around my shoulder in case I collapse.

But I feel okay. With Jack shepherding me, we walk slowly to the curb.

"They can't kill him!" someone says.

"Invincible Eddy!"

"Here we go," Jack says, and we step up on the sidewalk.

"Sorry, Jack," I say.

"That's okay."

"I didn't mean to cause you any trouble."

"Don't worry about that. Come on, let's go inside."

We walk into the Dusty Jacket. Jack sits me down at a table up front. His regulars come filing in. Outside, through the window, I see my truck still burning.

"Damn, Eddy," Jack says.

One of the regulars—a guy named Armstrong—says, "Hey Eddy, what'll you have? I'm buying."

"I'd take a shot of Johnnie Walker."

"Coming up," Jack says. He walks to the bar, where his other customers have settled on their stools again.

Armstrong says, "You're lucky to be in one piece."

"I don't know," I say. "I don't *feel* lucky."

Jack comes back with a shot of Johnnie Walker and a Shiner Bock. He puts them on the table in front of me.

"Thanks," I say. I thank Armstrong too. Lifting the shot, I salute them both before tossing it back. I put the glass down and drink some beer.

"Whoever rigged your truck, did it right out in the open, on the street," Jack says. "That took nerve. And probably more than one guy."

"I guess the price on my head went up again," I say.

"I'm wondering if this wasn't the Capalettis."

"Can I use your phone?" I say.

"Sure. You can use the one in my office. Come on."

I follow Jack toward the back. Next to the bathroom there's another door. Jack unlocks it, turns on a light, stands aside to let me in. It's like a closet with a desk in it. Wedged in with the desk and a chair are a filing cabinet and a safe. Every surface is covered with stacks of papers.

"Lock it when you're done," Jack says. He pulls the door shut.

CHAPTER 36

I SIT AT THE DESK. I find a phone book, open it, and flip through Restaurants until I see Casita Reynoso. They're closed, but it's the only way I can think of to get in touch with Maria.

I dial the number. The phone rings, then a guy says, "Hello? Casita Reynoso."

"Hi. I'm looking for Maria Juarez."

"We're closed."

"I really need to talk to her," I say.

"Maria's not here."

"Do you have a phone number for her?"

"You wait."

A woman gets on the phone. She says, "Who is calling, please?"

"This is Eddy Johnson. I was there this afternoon with Maria. I brought Raoul."

"Yes, I remember," the woman says. She must be the waitress who was polishing silverware with Maria—the tall older woman. Elena.

"I'm trying to get in touch with her," I say.

"She's at another job."

"Can I call her there?"

"Why so late?"

"Something's come up. It means I can get her more money. A lot more. But it can't wait."

"All right, I'll give you the number. Are you a nice man? You're not drunk, are you?"

"No, I'm just trying to help Maria."

"You sound drunk."

"Believe me, I'm stone cold sober."

"Okay. Here is the number." She calls it out to me. I write it on the palm of my left hand with a felt tip pen I find on the desk. When she's done, I read it back to her. "Yes," she says, adding, "You need to call, let it ring two times and hang up. Then call again."

"Okay. Thanks, Elena." I hang up.

I dial the number and do like she said. The second time I call, someone answers.

"Yo yo, what's up?"

"Raoul?" I say. "It's Eddy Johnson."

"What do *you* want?"

Someone else starts talking. Raoul holds the phone down and says something. Then Maria's on the line.

"Mr. Johnson?" she says. "How did you get this number?"

"Elena gave it to me."

"Why are you calling?"

"I need the other photograph."

"I don't understand."

"Big Frank says there were four."

"Yes, four. That's right."

"You only gave me three."

"That can't be, Mr. Johnson."

Neither one of us says anything. Then she says, "Hold on. Let me check something." She puts the phone down.

I take a swig of my Shiner Bock and look at my watch. It's a little after twelve-thirty. A hell of a day this has turned out to be. Not that it started well.

Maria comes back. "Mr. Johnson, I am so sorry. I don't know what to say."

"You have it?"

"It was still in my backpack. I was in a hurry when I put them in the bag, I guess."

"That's great news!"

"I feel like such an idiot."

"Don't. If it makes you feel better, Big Frank Miller got totally freaked out when he saw a photo was missing. It threw a real scare into him."

"Him and his scrawny daughter."

"The good news is, he's offering more money for it. I'll split it with you."

"I don't care about that. I mean, we can use the money. But I feel like I let you down. Raoul told me what happened at the house, how you stopped those men from kidnapping him. I am so grateful to you. Raoul is all I have."

"How soon can I get the photo?"

"I have to work till six a.m."

"Where are you? Can I come there?"

"Sure, I guess. I'm in the Addison Building, cleaning offices on the sixth floor."

"On 10th Street?"

"Yes. 10th and Armadillo."

"Okay, I'm coming over if that's all right."

"There's a pay phone outside the main entrance. When you get here, call me. Use the same signal, I'll come down and let you in."

"Thanks, Maria. See you soon."

I hang up and dial another number.

"Bernie's Bookshelves," some guy says.

"This is a friend of Bill's," I say.

The guy says, "How's the weather?"

"It's been raining so much there's puddles you could swim laps in."

"Hold on." There's a click, and Bill Holland comes on the line. "Yeah?" he says.

"Bill, it's Eddy."

"Eddy! You're alive!"

"Sure. Why not?"

"Word is you've got a terminal case of Luigi-itis."

"That's just a misunderstanding."

"Good. I've been waiting to hear from you. I owe you three hundred bucks. You were right about the Michener and the L'Amour."

"Oh. I forgot to check."

"I figured you were busy. What do you want to do? The Pulitzer Committee announces winners this Friday…"

"What are the odds-on Philip Roth?"

"Three-to-one."

"Put me down. All three hundred."

"Okay, three hundred on Roth. You got it. And Eddy, don't worry. If you win and something happens to you, I'll be sure and send nine hundred bucks worth of flowers to the funeral."

"Like there'd be a funeral. Listen. The reason I called: I need to get in touch with Joey."

"Oh yeah?"

"Tonight."

"Joey don't like me giving out his information."

"I really got to talk to him. I was with Sonny Cigalese tonight and he got killed. I need to tell Joey."

"I can get a message to him for you," Bill says. "That's all I can do. Where can Joey reach you?"

"I don't know. I can't go back to my room. I haven't figured out where I'm going. I guess just tell him I'll come by the warehouse in the morning."

"Okay. You take care of yourself, Eddy."

"Thanks, Bill."

I hang up.

CHAPTER 37

THERE'S A KNOCK on the office door. Jack leans his head in. He says, "Eddy, the police are here. They know it's your truck. They say you've got something to do with a couple cops getting killed... They're in a nasty mood. You need to give yourself up."

"How much time do I have?"

"Time's up, Eddy. There's a uniform out there now talking to my customers."

"Okay," I say.

"I don't want them to think I'm hiding you."

"Yeah, I get it."

"One minute," he says. He shuts the door and goes away.

I finish my beer—probably the last one I'll have for a while. I hate to give myself up, but Jack is right. The cops might mishandle me some if I'm in custody, but they're not as likely to shoot me.

When I'm ready, I open the door and walk out into the bar. Through the front window, the glow of my burning truck is gone. Instead there's the swirling lights of emergency vehicles livening up the night and the interior of the Dusty Jacket, dancing on the shoulders of the guys slumped on barstools.

Jack is wiping the bar top with a rag. He nods to me, but with an arched eyebrow that tells me someone is behind me.

A hand grabs my left arm.

"You Edward Johnson?" a cop says.

I half turn and see him. He's in uniform, his shoes all shiny—a fresh-scrubbed kid with a crew cut.

"Yes, that's me," I say.

"That your truck out there?"

"Which one?"

"Oh, I see," he says. "Hold your arms up." He searches me, finds Franco Capaletti's pistol, and takes it. "Okay, let's go," he says. He gives me a little push and we walk toward the bar's front door. He nods to Jack as we pass. Jack shrugs. "Sorry, Eddy," he says.

"It's okay."

Outside, the street is closed. There's a couple fire trucks, an EMS squad, six or seven police cars. They're parked this way and that. In the middle of everything is my charred truck, upside-down. It's still smoking. I can smell the burnt rubber of its tires. At either end of the block are wooden barricades and cops ready to hold pedestrians back. Not that many people are around at this hour.

One of the EMS guys is telling a cop, "There's no body. We even looked in the trees with flashlights."

We walk toward a fire truck. When we get close, I see Detective Jim Jernigan sitting on its back bumper, sipping from a cup of coffee. I'm glad to see him—the only Austin cop I trust. He's a good detective, tough and smart. I feed him tips sometimes. Nothing big.

The young cop leads me to Jernigan.

"Here he is, Detective."

Jernigan says, "Eddy! There you are!" He stands. "You're having yourself one hell of a night." He claps me on the shoulder.

"Good to see you, Jernigan," I say.

Jernigan says to the young cop, "Eddy here is one of my snitches."

"Hey!" I say.

"He had this on him," the young cop says, handing Jernigan Franco's gun.

"Ah," Jernigan says. "Thank you." He sniffs the gun. "Hasn't been fired this evening. Which is amazing, considering the shit storm you were in the middle of over at the Fiscal."

"Was I?" I say.

"Yes, and the brouhaha at your boardinghouse. Dead bodies all over the place, including two cops."

"Listen, Jernigan, I—"

"I don't want to hear it. Just be advised, Eddy. Your little spree is over. I'm taking you in."

"For what?"

"Oh, I don't know. Something will come to me. For now, let's just say it's to give the police department the rest of the night off. You leave one hell of a wake."

"But I haven't done anything."

"I did mention the two dead cops, didn't I? One of them had three kids. Three kids, Eddy."

I don't say anything.

"Cuff him," Jernigan tells the young cop. "Put him in my car."

I hold my wrists out. The cop puts cuffs on them.

He leads me to a police car and puts me in the back seat.

CHAPTER 38

AT THE POLICE STATION. Jernigan takes me to booking. He handcuffs me to a desk and leaves me there. Cops from different parts of the room keep throwing me dirty looks. I'm somehow part of how two cops got killed tonight, and there's nothing these guys take more personally. I feel exposed sitting handcuffed in their midst, like bobbing in shark-infested waters.

It's one-thirty when Jernigan comes back. He sits at the desk, gets a blank form from a drawer, feeds it into the typewriter, and starts typing—entering preliminaries.

Then, pausing, he looks up at me. "Okay," he says. "Let's see if we can get through this without you making me want to hit you. Because, so help me, Eddy, I might. And I'm not sure how I'd stop."

"Am I under arrest?"

"Let's just say you've got some explaining to do… What happened at your boardinghouse?"

"I went to my room about seven-thirty. Sonny Cigalese was with me."

"And the reason he was with you?"

"For protection. Joey Romano loaned him to me as like a bodyguard."

"Why would you need protection?"

"Luigi Capaletti put a price on my head."

There's no place on the form for Jernigan to put all this stuff. He takes a sip of coffee, then says, "Okay, I'm just going to keep going. Why would Luigi Capaletti put a price on your head?"

"Because I shot his son."

"*You're* the guy that shot Franco Capaletti?"

"Twice, actually—both times accidents. It's just a misunderstanding."

"Jesus, Eddy."

"The two guys that showed up at the boardinghouse were trying to kill me, so Sonny shot them. In self-defense. Same thing with the guy on the eighteenth floor of the Fiscal—the guy dressed up like room service."

Jernigan thinks a little, does some typing, then says, "Okay, so that explains all those dead guys. What about the cops?"

"That never should have happened. We were crossing the lobby, leaving the hotel, when this detective stopped us. He recognized Sonny."

"He's kind of tough to miss."

"Right. So he stopped us. But instead of waiting for backup or playing it easy, he got up in Sonny's face and started pushing his buttons. I don't know why he did that. Sonny shot him twice point blank. He was dead before he hit the ground. Then the other cop and Sonny started shooting and killed each other. When it was over, I got up and ran. I went to where my truck was but when I tried to start it, it blew up. Then you hauled me in here."

Jernigan sits back in his chair thinking. "I don't know, Eddy," he says. "You make it seem like you're just a witness. The problem is, it looks like I've got a gang war breaking out and you're the common denominator."

"Well, I shot Franco Capaletti. But, like I said, those were accidents."

Jernigan brings his fist down on top of the desk hard. The typewriter jumps a little. I jump too.

"Damnit, Eddy!"

"It's the truth!"

Jernigan calms himself. He says, "Let me tell you how it looks to me. It seems nuts, but it's the only way things fit together. To start with, you're down and out. A two-bit dealer. Living in a flea-bag boardinghouse, peddling literature nobody cares about. Then you need some money. You get a girlfriend, you bet too much on the wrong bestseller. Something. Next thing I know, you're palling around with Joey Romano, going after the Capalettis."

"It's not like that," I say. "I'm on my own. I just needed a favor from Joey is all. And there's no war."

"Maybe you haven't heard. You've been so busy. There was another shootout tonight. Some of Luigi's boys ambushed Tony D'Adderio. They got him coming out of the Walden's in Round Rock."

Tony Hey-Ho D'Adderio. One of Joey's top guys. Hell, maybe a war *is* breaking out. Maybe, by shooting Franco, I'm like the cow that kicked that lantern over in Chicago.

Jernigan sees I am surprised. He says, "I'm trying to help you out, Eddy. But let me tell you. We're going to hold you responsible for a whole lot more than just those two dead cops if you don't come clean. I'll fix it so you won't be able to sell a Harlequin Romance in this city."

"I'm trying to cooperate. If I tell you the truth and you don't believe me, what can I do?"

"Why'd you go see Big Frank Miller?" he says. "Are Joey and Miller in cahoots?"

"No! They don't even know each other!"

A detective, one I don't know, comes up to Jernigan holding a file. "Can I see you a minute?" he says.

Jernigan stands and walks off a distance with the detective. As they talk, the detective opens the file and shows Jernigan something. Jernigan takes the file. He flips through it, stopping here and there. The detective walks away.

Jernigan comes back to the desk holding the file. He doesn't sit.

"Well, Eddy," he says. "The ballistics just came back from your gun. You want the good news first, or the bad news?"

I don't say anything. He's talking about Franco Capaletti's pistol, but the tone he's taking, I decide to keep my mouth shut.

"The good news is, we've just solved an execution-style murder from two years ago. And who knows how many more. They're matching your ballistics against a whole stack of cold cases.

"The bad news is, it looks like you might be headed for death row: killing time until you ride old sparky... What's the matter? Got nothing clever to say?"

I act like I don't.

"You know, Eddy, you've had us fooled for a long time. We

never even noticed you. Living at the Alamo like you did—that was genius."

"I'm done talking," I say. "Give me my phone call. I want to talk to my attorney."

"At this point, that's probably a good idea. Here, you can use this." He swings a phone around and puts it close enough that I can use it while cuffed to the desk. "I'm going to go let the boys in Homicide know what's up. You'll be dealing with them from here on out."

"Hey, Warmus!" he says to a cop a couple desks over. "You gonna be here a while?"

"Sure."

"You know who this guy is?"

"Yeah, he's connected to what happened at the Fiscal."

"Keep an eye on him. I'll be back in ten minutes."

"No problem," Warmus says.

Jernigan walks away. I watch him until he turns a corner. Then I notice Warmus has come over. He's standing next to me. I don't know him. He's younger, but he seems intense.

"You scumbag," he says.

I think he's going to take a swing at me, and I cringe. I'm cuffed to the desk, so there's not much I can do about it.

"Don't worry," he says. "I'm not going to hit you." He leans in close and says quietly, so nobody else can hear, "Luigi says hello, Eddy." Then he *does* hit me, landing a left hook against the side of my head. It hurts like hell.

I brace for more, but he's already done, walking back to his desk. He sits. When he sees me looking at him, he gives me the finger.

CHAPTER 39

I SCOOT MY CHAIR CLOSER to the desk and pull the phone toward me. I dial the number for Maria written on my hand, then hang up and call again.

Maria answers. "Mr. Johnson. Are you downstairs?"

"No. The cops picked me up. I'm at the police station."

"They arrested you?"

"Not yet. That might be next. I'm in a lot of trouble, Maria. I didn't tell you before: someone blew up my truck tonight."

"That's terrible! Are you okay?"

"Yeah, I'm fine. But the sooner I get that photo, the better. I'm hoping the cops will release me sometime tomorrow. Where can I call you if I get out?"

"Call Casita Reynoso. If I'm not there, you can talk to Elena."

"Okay."

"I wish there were some way I could get the photo to you tonight. Can you have visitors?"

"I don't think so."

"I'm going to try, Mr. Johnson. If that doesn't work, I'll wait to hear from you tomorrow."

"I appreciate it."

"It's the least I can do. I feel terrible about all this."

"Thanks, Maria."

I hang up.

I dial the number for Harry's Bar. It rings a few times, then there's lots of noise—loud music and people talking. "Yeah," a guy's voice says. "Harry's Bar."

"Harry," I say. "It's Eddy Johnson."

"Eddy. You're alive!"

I say, "Is Abernathy there?"

"You know he is."

"Put him on, will you?"

"Sure thing, Eddy." I hear him shouting over the noise in the bar, "Henry! It's Eddy!"

"Here he comes," Harry says to me. "Good luck, Eddy."

The phone gets handed over.

"Mr. Johnson," Abernathy says. "Esteemed client. Worthy fellow. It is an honor to hear from you."

"Abernathy," I say. "I'm at the police station. They're going to arrest me."

"No!" Abernathy holds the phone away from his mouth and says—to Harry, I guess— "Edward is in the hands of the police." He talks into the phone again. "How can this be? That a man of your integrity and standing should be challenged, much less detained—your enterprising spirit ensnared…"

"Abernathy!" I say.

"And that such misfortune should befall you at a time when you are in debt to your attorney…"

"I've got your money, Abernathy. I've got it with me, in cash. The two hundred I owe you plus another two hundred for tonight. I'll pay you when you get here."

"How savvy of you. How keen your understanding of our great nation's system of justice. Our founding fathers, if they were here, would no doubt—"

"Come get me out of here, Abernathy."

"Ex post facto, Mr. Johnson. One quick toast to your good name and off I go. I shall pry loose the gripping talons, undo the coiling tentacles. Whatever it is you have done, no matter the evidence against you, we will have you free in no time, you have my solemn pledge."

"Abernathy," I say. "Drink some coffee or something. Splash some water on your face."

But he's talking to Harry again. "A double, my good man. For soon I will be grappling with the enforcers. Horn-to-horn, it will be. Tusk-to-tusk."

I hang up.

CHAPTER 40

JERNIGAN COMES BACK. He uncuffs me from the desk, gets me to my feet, and cuffs my hands again.

"Come on," he says, pushing me ahead of him through the big room. It's mostly empty. The few cops on duty, each at a desk, look up and scowl at me as I go by.

"Where are we going?" I say.

"I'm taking you to an interview room, so we can have a little privacy."

We come to a long hallway and follow it to the right. Jernigan stops in front of a door marked A-36. He opens the door and ushers me into a room with no windows—a blank white cube containing a big wooden table and chairs. A light bulb is screwed into the ceiling. It's a mean little room, where questions get asked a lot of ways, and answers aren't always enough.

"Take a seat, Eddy," Jernigan says.

I go around the table and sit, facing the door.

"Are you going to uncuff me?" I say.

"No, I don't think so." He's still standing. "You've got visitors."

There's a knock on the door. Jernigan opens it.

"Come in," he says. A woman steps into the room—handsome, somewhere in her forties, with streaks of gray and a regal manner. She's wearing a bright blue pantsuit with big lapels, a white silk blouse, and a pendant necklace that looks like a gnarl of petrified wood or maybe a tribal whistle.

"Is this him?" she says to Jernigan, meaning me.

"His name is Eddy Johnson."

She's such a showboat, at first I don't notice the guy with her. He's maybe a decade younger, dressed casually, all in black. He's small but with an athleticism, a kind of coiled grace.

"Thank you, Detective," the woman says. "That will be all." Jernigan leaves the room, shutting the door behind him.

"Mr. Johnson," she says. She sits across from me, puts a blue leather clasp on the table. "I'm Maxine Anderson. I'm with the Committee to Re-Elect Mayor Travis."

I don't say anything.

"This is Derek, my assistant."

I look at the guy, but he doesn't reciprocate. Standing behind Maxine Anderson's chair, he's as still and calm as fallen snow.

"It's an honor," I tell her. "I'd shake your hand if I didn't have these cuffs on."

"I understand. Yes, apparently you're in quite a lot of trouble." She hesitates, not sure how to say what's on her mind.

"It's your meeting," I say.

"Yes, of course. Mr. Johnson, I think you have something that belongs to the mayor."

"What would that be?"

"I think you know exactly the thing I mean."

"Oh yeah?"

She says, "Perhaps it would make a difference if I mentioned the mayor is willing to pay a significant amount of money for its return."

I shrug.

"His honor will pay two thousand dollars for it."

"Here's the thing, Maxine. The mayor would already have the item he wants if he'd paid two thousand dollars for it yesterday. He said he would. But instead he double-crossed the seller. So now he doesn't have what he wants, and the people that do have it don't trust him. Not to get too technical, but that makes him shit out of luck."

"Four thousand," she says.

"You're missing the point, Maxine."

Derek says quietly, "Call her Ms. Anderson."

"It's okay, Derek," Maxine says. "Mr. Johnson, I appreciate the point you're making. It seems to me a bit of an overreaction."

"Really? I've been shot at more times in the last two days than a tin duck on the State Fair midway. Someone blew up my truck, and now I'm in jail accused of murder. And why? Because his honor decided to send some goons to steal the item instead of paying for it."

"I assure you, those individuals were provided the requisite funds and instructed to perform the transaction as agreed. Mayor Travis in no way approved of, nor would he ever condone, violence of any kind."

"So, what you're saying is, the mayor's a really good guy but he has bad judgment. It comes to the same thing as far as I'm concerned. He should have sent you and Derek."

"I wish he had," Maxine says.

Derek says, "We're here now."

"Right. The thing is—and I don't know, maybe it's different in politics—but in my business a deal, if anything goes wrong with it, it's not a deal anymore. It's dead."

"Nonsense," Maxine says. "Six thousand."

"I'm not negotiating," I say.

"You've already sold it to someone else?"

"Maybe, maybe not. Either way, it's not for sale to *you*."

"Very well… You surprise me, Mr. Johnson."

She opens her blue leather clasp, gets a business card, and puts it on the table in front of me. "This is my card. If you change your mind, contact me. I'm sure we can work together to everyone's satisfaction. I am prepared to pay ten thousand dollars, by the way. Just so you know. Before the election, of course."

She stands, ready to go, but hesitates and says, "Big Frank Miller is a real estate developer, that's all. He has a lot of money and some charm, but he is not a politician. He has no interest in public service."

"I get it," I say. "I know all about his downtown development plans. He's going to demolish the building I live in."

"What building is that?"

"The Alamo Boardinghouse."

Her eyebrows go up. "I see… Well, you take care, Mr. Johnson. Derek," she says. He opens the door. She leaves the room, then he does, shutting the door behind him.

I stuff the card in one of my pockets.

CHAPTER 41

SITTING IN THE ROOM CUFFED, waiting for Jernigan to come back, I remember something. A public defender told me years ago: *Admit nothing. The difference between what they know and what they can prove is all you have and might be all you need.*

Someone knocks on the door.

"Housekeeping," a woman says.

"Someone's in here," I say.

The door opens and a big metal cart full of cleaning equipment and supplies comes in. It's like a Zamboni, with a mop and broom sticking up in front. It barely fits through the door, and it's hardly inside the room when it bumps into the chair Maxine was sitting in, pushing it against the table. The table starts moving toward me. If it doesn't stop, I'll be shoved up against the wall.

"Hey, look out," I say.

"Sorry, I need to clean the room."

The woman closes the room's door and comes around from behind the cart. Maria Juarez!

"Maria?" I say.

"They said no visitors."

Packages of paper towels on the cart's bottom shelf move, then slide out and fall to the floor. A head emerges. It's Raoul. He crawls off the cart and stands.

"Heya, Mr. Johnson," he says. He looks around at the room, sees my handcuffs. "Gee, I guess you really are in a jam."

"Do you have an attorney?" Maria says.

"Not a good one."

She grabs a plastic spray bottle with a pink antiseptic solution in it from the cart and starts spritzing the table. She wipes the table with a cloth towel. "I'm just going to keep cleaning in case someone comes in," she says.

"How did you get in here?"

"I just walked in. I borrowed the cart from my other job."

"I'm impressed."

"If you tell people you've come to clean, they're not likely to send you away."

"You pushed it here?"

She nods.

"Those sidewalks were bumpy," Raoul says. "Did someone really blow up your truck?"

"Yes."

"Were you in it when it happened?"

Maria says, "That's enough, Raoul." She reaches in her apron pocket and pulls out a Polaroid photograph. "Here is the photo," she says, putting it face down on the table in front of me.

As I reach for it, she says, "If it makes you puke, I'm not cleaning it up."

I pick it up and turn it over. "I'm not gonna—" I say, but, looking at the photo, I shut up.

Maria has somehow managed to save the wildest one for last.

"Jesus," I say

"He is *Pig* Frank Miller."

Maria spits on the table, then spritzes it with the spray bottle and wipes it clean.

I put the photo in my jacket's breast pocket.

"Thanks," I say.

"It's the least I can do. I'm not cut out to be a criminal. As much as I hate the Millers, I'm sorry I took the stuff."

"On the other hand," I say, reaching into my pants pocket for the roll of money Big Frank gave me, "it turns out crime does sometimes pay, even if it's wrong."

I take the rubber band from around the money and open the roll up. Fifty one-hundred-dollar bills. I count out twenty-five and offer them to Maria.

"Courtesy of the Millers," I say.

"How much is that?" Raoul says.

"Twenty-five hundred."

Maria doesn't take the money. "Are you sure?" she says.

"You've earned it."

She takes the money. "Thank you, Mr. Johnson. This is very generous of you."

"There might be even more," I say. "We'll see."

She puts the money in her apron pocket. I put my share away too.

"I hope you get out of here soon," she says. She puts the spray bottle and towel back on the cart and tells Raoul, "Come on. It's time to go."

"See you, Eddy," Raoul says. "Good luck."

"Bye, Raoul."

He gets down low and crawls onto the bottom shelf of the cart. Maria puts the paper towels on the shelf to hide him. Then she stands up straight, adjusts her cleaning uniform.

"Well, Mr. Eddy," she says. "Thanks again. Come by the restaurant sometime."

The door opens and Jernigan comes in with another detective.

"What the hell?" he says, seeing the cleaning cart and Maria, in her uniform, standing next to it. "Who are you?"

"Cleaning."

"What are you doing here?"

She says, "I done."

He shakes his head. "Okay. Here, let me help you." He pulls on the end of the cart facing him as Maria pushes from behind, and they get the cart out into the hallway.

"Gracias," Maria says.

She heads down the hall with the cart.

CHAPTER 42

JERNIGAN COMES BACK IN THE ROOM and shuts the door. He and the other detective sit in chairs across from me.

"Eddy," Jernigan says. "This is Detective Krygowski from Homicide. He's the lead detective on your case."

"Either of you guys got a candy bar?"

"Maybe we can get you one later," Jernigan says. "We need to get down to business."

"No more time for visitors, Jernigan?" I look him in the eye as I say it. It makes him uncomfortable.

"We'll ask the questions, Johnson," Krygowski says.

"Where's my attorney?"

"I don't know," Jernigan says. "But listen. You called Abernathy, right?"

I nod.

"He can't help you, Eddy. Parking tickets is more his speed."

"He's better than nothing."

"Maybe."

"Anyway, that gun you ran ballistics on isn't mine."

"We know that," Krygowski says.

"You do?"

"Uniforms took *your* gun from you yesterday, over on the east side."

"That's right!"

"That doesn't change anything," Krygowski says. "The pistol we took off you in the Dusty Jacket is tied to an execution-style killing out in Wimberly—at least that's where we found the body. The serial number is scratched out, so it's anonymous."

"It's a game of musical holsters, Eddy, and you lose."

"You're going to frame me?"

"You're good enough for it," Krygowski says.

"This is bullshit."

"Lie down with gangsters, wake up doing ten-to-twenty, Eddy," Jernigan says.

"How am I going to know when my lawyer shows? Maybe I should wait alone."

"Don't worry, they'll bring him here."

"Well, I'm done talking."

"No problem," Jernigan says. "How about instead you listen? There's no harm in that… Now, I filled in Krygowski as to how you do a little snitching for me."

"Why do you have to call it that?"

"Okay. You're an informant. Is that better?"

He's trying to pull me into a conversation, but I know better. I keep my mouth shut.

"Anyway, you've cooperated with the police before, so you know how it works. We get something, you get something. Up to now, it's been small-time stuff. But you've come up, Eddy.

You're in the big leagues now."

"Dead-Eye Eddy," Krygowski says.

"You're in a lot of trouble. I'm still not clear on how you managed it."

He pauses in case I feel like explaining. I look back at him, no expression on my face.

"Just to make sure we're on the same page," he says, "the Capalettis have ten grand on your head. You're a person of interest in a shooting that claimed the lives of two cops. It's a miracle you weren't killed when your truck blew up. We got you on the hook for this Wimberly thing. And word on the street is Joey Romano is pissed at you."

"You're screwed," Krygowski says. "How long you think you'll last on the streets if we cut you loose?"

"I'll take my chances."

Jernigan says to Krygowski, "I don't think we should release Eddy without keeping an eye on him. We'd feel terrible if something should happen."

"Yeah, when his luck runs out."

"We could surveil him."

"Discreetly," Krygowski says.

I'm watching these guys; they're doing a whole routine. I figure why interrupt?

"We could be his guardian angels," Jernigan says. "What worries me, though, is if he does get in trouble—if he gets in a jam—how would we know? Afterwards, sure. We'd find his body. But I mean when there's still time to save him."

"I know," Krygowski says. "He could wear a wire. That way we could listen in. He could use a code word if he's in danger."

"That's a great idea," Jernigan says.

"You guys are funny," I say.

"And if, by chance, someone should incriminate themselves while they're talking to him…"

"Sure," I say, "I could hang out with criminals and say stuff like, *Hey, you guys committed any crimes lately? Tell me all the details.*"

"If the crimes were serious enough, and the individuals important enough, we might be able to get you into the Witness Protection Program."

"Okay. But what if something goes wrong? Have you got a Witness Resurrection Program?"

"You'll have better odds working with us than being on your own."

"Maybe. My problem is I have this independent streak. I'm like a desperado."

"You better come to your senses, Eddy."

"I should let somebody love me?"

There's a knock on the door.

"Yeah," Krygowski says over his shoulder.

"Guy's lawyer's here," a cop says.

Another voice, a rich booming baritone I've never heard before, says, "I demand to see my client this instant. His rights have been trampled long enough."

The cops must have got their signals crossed, brought somebody else's lawyer to this room by mistake. Whoever he is, he sounds ten times as authoritative as Abernathy. And ten times as expensive.

"I'll call the governor if I have to," the lawyer shouts. "Don't play games that could cost you your careers."

Jernigan is looking at me. "You called Abernathy," he says.

"I know. I don't know who this guy is."

"You got the wrong room," Jernigan shouts.

"Edward?" the lawyer says. "Edward Johnson? Call out to me! Are you in there? Let me hear your voice."

"Christ," Jernigan says. He shouts, "Let him in."

CHAPTER 43

THE DOOR OPENS and the attorney comes rushing in. He's an older guy—distinguished looking but also huge: with thick arms and legs and a portly stomach. He's wearing a three-piece suit.

He hurries to my side.

"Edward," he says. "Good dear Edward." He places a thick pink hand on my shoulder and confronts the detectives.

"Whatever half-baked charges you have the gall to bring against this man, state them now."

"What are you doing here, Burnell?" Jernigan says.

"The question, my dear detective, is rather: *what is Edward doing here?*"

I don't know this Burnell guy, but I'm catching on fast that he could be my ticket out of here.

"They never even arrested me," I say. "They're trying to frame me for a murder."

"You shut up," Jernigan says. His face is flushed. "You son of a bitch. You lied to me."

"Now now, Detective," Burnell says.

"I told you the truth, Jernigan."

"Silence is golden," Burnell says, giving my shoulder a squeeze.

Jernigan says, "Sure, Eddy. You're just a guy on his own. And if you get in a jam, this piece of garbage just happens to show up in the middle of the night. Joey Romano's personal attorney."

Jernigan is furious. A vein is throbbing in his forehead.

I turn and look at Burnell. He's totally relaxed.

"Are you Joey Romano's attorney?" I say.

"Perhaps. But I am here to represent *your* interests."

Krygowski says, "Come on, Johnson. Drop the act."

"I have no idea why Joey Romano would send this guy to spring me. I'm as surprised as you are."

"Screw you, Eddy," Jernigan says. "You scum-sucking low-life dirtbag."

"Well now, detectives," Burnell says. "If you have exhausted your limited vocabulary, perhaps the grinding ahead of justice can resume. I believe you became hysterical and disruptive when I asked what charges are to be brought against this man."

"You dirty shyster," Jernigan says.

"That then—if I understand police idiom as I think I do—translates roughly to *there are no charges, he's free to go*?"

"Yeah, he can go."

Krygowski says, "You won't last twenty-four hours, Johnson. You're dead! Dead!"

"Edward, you are released," Burnell says. "Let us leave behind this place."

"Jernigan," I say.

He's staring at me. He says, "The Capalettis are gonna take good care of you, Eddy. If they don't, I will."

"On your feet," Burnell says. I stand. I hold my hands out, Jernigan comes around the table with a little key and unlocks the cuffs. He drops them on the table.

I'm rubbing my wrists when Jernigan, still looking at me, says to Burnell, "Tell Joey he should be careful. Eddy here's a snitch."

"Once a rat, always a rat," Krygowski says.

I say, "Come on, you guys. Now you're just making stuff up."

Burnell walks to the door and opens it. "Come, Edward," he says, stepping out of the room.

I walk to the open doorway.

"I'll call you, Jernigan," I say, but he and Krygowski have turned away, waiting for me to be gone.

I walk out of the room. I find Burnell a few yards ahead slurping at a water fountain. When he's done, he straightens up, dabbing at his mouth with a folded handkerchief.

"Ah," he says, seeing me. He gives me a smile and claps me on the back. We walk together up the corridor toward the lobby.

"I must say, Edward. You need to learn to stand up for yourself."

"I'm not used to having an attorney who can call the governor."

"Yes, of course. But remember: the police are nearly always bluffing."

I nod.

We get to the lobby, a high-ceilinged room with marble floors and wooden benches, tall arched windows full of darkness. There's a slight tint of blue in the night sky—dawn on its way.

Outside the front entrance, a black Lincoln is waiting, exhaust coming from its tailpipe.

"My ride," Burnell says.

"Thanks for springing me."

"I have a message for you from Mr. Romano."

"What?"

"I have no idea," he says. He pulls an envelope from his jacket's breast pocket and hands it to me. My name is written on the front.

Burnell says, "And now I bid you adieu." He pushes the front doors open and goes outside.

I open the envelope, pull a piece of paper out and read: *Jesus, Eddy. Come by the warehouse. We're all here.*

CHAPTER 44

WHEN I LOOK UP, Burnell is in the back seat of the Lincoln, pulling his door shut. The Lincoln takes off. I toss Joey's note in a trash can and go outside. I walk down the steps to the sidewalk.

A few cars go by, including two cop cars that turn into the police station parking lot. A Yellow Cab turns onto 8th Street one block east and comes toward me. I go to the curb, raise my arm to flag it down, and it stops. The front window on my side slides down.

I lean down to get a look at the driver. He's bearded, wearing a turban. "Good morning," he says, nodding to me. "You are needing a ride?"

"Yes."

"Please, get in. I will take you."

I get in the back of the cab.

"Where are we going?" the driver says

"Romano Brothers, on 2nd Street."

"The warehouse district. Yes... Very good, sir." He hits the meter and pulls away from the curb, heading toward Congress

Avenue. We hang a left on Congress and go past the Fiscal Hotel. It's calm there—like nothing happened.

Dawn is breaking. I'm exhausted. I yawn, feeling again how hungry I am. We turn east on 2nd and enter the warehouse district, bumping over railroad tracks.

Just past the intersection with Trinity, the driver pulls to the side of the road and stops.

"What's going on?" I say.

"I think I may have a flat."

"I didn't feel anything."

"It might just be low. I need to take a look." He opens his door. "I won't be a minute, sir." He gets out.

"Wait," I say, but he doesn't hear me. He's running down 2nd Street as fast as he can. He didn't even shut his door.

An unmarked white Chevy van with no rear windows comes along, pulls over in front of the cab, and stops.

Two guys get out of the van and walk back toward me. Certified Grade A thugs, big and serious, wearing cheap suits. One of them has a sawed-off shotgun leveled at me through the cab's windshield.

He watches me while the other guy comes around and opens my door.

"Okay, Johnson," he says. "Let's go."

I get out of the cab.

"Hold still," he says, and he pats me down, making sure I don't have a gun.

"Who are you guys?" I say. "What do you want?"

"We don't want anything," the guy with the shotgun says. "We're making a delivery."

"Can we take the cab, Manny?" the other guy says. "I hate this van."

"Yeah, I don't care. You want to drive?"

"Sure." He goes around the cab to the open driver's door, gets in behind the wheel.

Manny says, "Okay. Now you. In front."

I open the front passenger door of the cab and get in. Manny shuts my door and gets in behind me.

"Just take it easy, Roy," he says. "There's no hurry."

CHAPTER 45

ROY PUTS THE CAB IN GEAR, makes a wide, slow U-turn, and heads west on 2nd Street.

"Where are we going?" I say.

"To see a certain pal of yours," Roy says.

"You called me Johnson," I say. "I don't know who you think I am, but my name is Mark Maxwell. I'm visiting from Abilene."

"Yeah, right," Manny says behind me.

Roy laughs. "Glad to meet you," he says. "I'm Santa Claus."

"I only mention it because I get the feeling whoever you work for might get mad when he finds out you got the wrong guy."

"Shut the hell up," Manny says. "We heard all about you and your tricks."

"What if he's telling the truth?" Roy says.

"It's him all right."

Nobody says anything for a while. It's dawn. When we get to Congress Avenue, the streetlights go off. An All-American Statesman truck is in front of Pappy's kiosk—a guy slinging bundles of the morning edition onto the sidewalk. We turn left and head toward the river. The closer we get to the bridge, the more certain I am these guys are with the Capalettis.

I say, "You know, you guys are both accessories to murder if you hand me over to Luigi."

"Don't worry about that," Manny says. "We're not a couple of boy scouts never got our hands dirty."

"Yeah, we already got our murder merit badge," Roy says.

"Good one, Roy."

We cross the bridge. I see the convention center. We go by the Nighthawk Diner—best biscuits in the city, and I wouldn't mind some, slathered with strawberry jam and butter, on a platter with a cheese omelet and thick sliced bacon…

We turn left on Riverside Drive. The Capalettis' warehouse is just a few miles ahead.

I say, "Listen, you guys. You let me go—just pull over to the side of the road and let me out—I'll make it worth your while. Twenty-five hundred bucks. What do you say?"

"And what do we tell Luigi?" Roy says.

Manny says, "You got that kind of money?"

"Sure."

"Let me see."

"It's in my pants."

"Reach slow," he says.

I scoot forward on the car's seat and reach down inside my pants pocket. I pull out my half of the five grand I split with Maria. I hold it up so Manny can see it.

"Give it here," he says. I reach the money back and he takes it. I hear him counting it.

"Twenty-five hundred," he says. "Thanks. It won't do you

any good where you're going."

"What the hell," I say.

Roy says, "Way to go, Manny."

"After we drop him, we'll split it."

We're maybe six blocks from the Capalettis' warehouse. I say, "Come on, guys. A deal's a deal."

"Aw, shut up," Manny says. "Because of you, Franco's in the hospital."

Coming up on the left side of the road, I see the warehouse— an imposing brick building. A sign on its north wall says:

Capaletti and Son Books
Serving South Austin since 1963
Your reading needs and more.

Above the building—across a massive scaffold rising from the building's roof—there's a giant neon book that opens and closes, opens and closes. It's not turned on.

We turn left into the parking lot and drive around to the back.

CHAPTER 46

ROY PULLS UP TO a drive-in door in back of the warehouse and honks the horn. The door starts going up. We drive inside the warehouse.

We're in a huge open room—mostly aisles of metal skid rack. To our left is a row of loading docks, ten or twelve of them, with dock plates and pallet jacks scattered here and there. A forklift is parked at the end.

By the time we get out of the cab, the overhead door is closed. The guy who closed it comes over. Another huge guy. Where do they get them all?

"So, this is Dead-Eye Eddy," he says.

"Yep," Manny says.

"He don't look so scary."

"He's a weasel. But a weasel can wipe out your chickens same as an eagle. Get me some zip ties, will ya?"

The guy goes to a supply cart and grabs some zip ties. Manny hands the guy the shotgun and takes the ties.

"Hold out your hands," he tells me. He ties my wrists

together nice and tight, then takes the shotgun back.

"Let's go," he says, poking me with the end of the gun. "Time to see Luigi."

We walk to a man door next to a time clock and a rack of punch cards. Roy opens the door, and we step into a well-lit carpeted hallway with a low drop ceiling. We walk to a wooden door at the end of the hallway, Manny behind me with the shotgun, Roy behind him. Roy steps forward and knocks on the door.

"Come in," a man's voice says.

Roy opens the door, and we go into an office. It's big and plain—white wallboard, cheap blue carpet, a drop ceiling with inset fluorescent lighting. There's a desk and matching bookcases with cherry veneer. The office has an impersonal suburban feel.

In contrast, Luigi is ancient, weathered and marked by time, his hands and face gnarled. Sitting in a wheelchair parked next to the desk, he looks like an archaeological relic. A thin oxygen tank is strapped to the wheelchair behind him, a clear plastic tube connected to his nostrils.

I had no idea he was so old. I almost feel sorry for him. He's wearing cheerful cruise wear, a bright red shirt patterned with palm trees, but there's no getting around the grim fact that he's not long for this world. On the other hand, his eyes are not milky and out of focus like my grandfather's before he died. They're sharp and hard, glinting like gems. He is staring at me furiously.

"This is the guy that shot Franco," Manny says.

Luigi says, "Bring him here." Manny and Roy walk me closer, until we're right in front of the wheelchair, standing over it. Manny puts the shotgun down on top of the desk.

"You," Luigi says. He lifts a hand and points at me with a

crooked arthritic finger, jabbing as he speaks. "You tried to kill my Franco. You and Joey Romano. But you made a big mistake."

"I never meant to shoot him, Mr. Capaletti. I had no idea who he was. I've got nothing but respect for you and your family."

"Manny! Slap him!"

Manny jerks me around, swings his arm, and slaps me across the face with the thick palm of his hand. It hurts like hell.

Luigi says, "I put a hit on you, but I changed my mind. Franco needs to be the one who takes you out. So he can get his mojo back."

I don't say anything. My face is stinging from Manny's slap.

"Tomorrow, Joey's going to find you, and then he'll know. He's finished."

"Mr. Capaletti," I say.

"Slap him again!"

Manny slaps me. Now my head is throbbing, my eyes watering.

"Yeah, doesn't feel too good, does it?" Luigi says. He laughs. "When Franco gets back from the hospital, you're dogmeat. I don't know how you got over on him. I look at you, I can see you're nothing but a punk. But you've become a dark cloud over his head. A shadow on his path. You put some bullets in him, but let me tell you something, it takes a lot more than that to kill a Capaletti. You should have…"

Luigi's eyes close and his mouth goes slack. His head falls forward. He slumps in the wheelchair.

"Oh shit," Manny says. "Roy, check his oxygen."

Roy goes behind the wheelchair and looks at the gauge on top of the tank. "It's empty," he says.

"Get another one. They're in the closet, over there."

Roy hurries to the closet, gets a tank, and carries it to the wheelchair. Luigi is still out cold. He's not moving. I can hear his breath, but it's strained and shallow.

Roy fumbles with the empty tank but he doesn't know how to unhook it. "Damn it," he says.

"Jesus, Roy," Manny says. "Here, take Dead-Eye. I'll do it."

Roy comes over and grabs one of my arms. Manny goes behind Luigi and, using a key hanging from a chain, twists the regulator off the top of the empty tank. He unstraps the tank and replaces it with the full one. He gets the regulator hooked up, then opens the nozzle all the way. I hear oxygen flowing.

We all wait, watching Luigi. I'm sure Manny and Roy are hoping they don't have to do CPR on him. Pretty soon his breathing gets stronger—more relaxed and regular. He's getting what he needs. He stirs, then sits up, his eyes not quite focused. Slowly, he comes back to himself.

"Are you okay, Luigi?" Manny says.

"I'm fine. Why? What happened?"

"You ran out of oxygen."

"What are you talking about? I don't need that stuff. I only keep it around so my wife don't worry."

Manny comes around the wheelchair and stands next to me. I have him on one side, Roy on the other.

"Where's Franco?" Luigi says.

"He's on his way," Manny says. "He just got out of the hospital."

"That's right," Luigi says. "Because of you..." He's staring at me again. "You put him there... Manny! Stomp on his foot!"

Manny lifts a leg and slams his foot down on my left foot.

He's wearing a low-heeled shoe, but not low enough. It hurts so bad I scream and fall to the carpet. "Get him up," Luigi says. Manny and Roy pull me to my feet.

"Do it again!"

I try to move, but Roy hugs me tight and Manny stomps on the same foot again. I scream some more.

"Hold him!" Luigi says. With both hands he pushes his wheelchair's big wheels, rolling toward me. Manny and Roy hold me tight. Luigi turns the wheelchair and, leaning over to see, rolls one wheel until it's next to my left foot, which is throbbing and hurts like hell.

"Vendetta!" he shouts. He rolls the wheel, bumping it up on top of my foot, and puts the handbrake on. I scream, wriggling like a fish on a hook, Manny and Roy still holding me. I somehow have the strength to lift my foot against the wheel that's causing such pain, and the wheel lifts with it. The wheelchair flips over, dumping Luigi out onto the carpet. I stop screaming and the room goes silent. I hear a soft whimpering from Luigi, who lies curled in a fetal position behind the toppled wheelchair.

"Boss!" Manny says. He goes to Luigi, gets down on his knees next to him. "Boss! Are you okay?"

"Do I look like I'm okay?" Luigi says. "I think I broke my wrist. It snapped! Shit!" he yells in frustration and pain, trying to sit up but refusing Manny's help.

CHAPTER 47

THE DOOR TO THE OFFICE OPENS and Franco comes in wearing a red velour track suit and white sneakers. His one hand is bandaged and he's favoring the leg I shot.

He takes in the tableau we are—Luigi writhing on the floor near the overturned wheelchair; Manny on his knees next to him, helpless; me in zip ties, Roy holding my arm.

"You!" Franco yells, meaning me. "What have you done to my father? Papa!" he says, lurching toward Luigi. "Papa! Are you okay?"

"He broke my wrist," Luigi says.

Manny gets up and steps back to make room for Franco, who is working his way with difficulty down to the carpet near Luigi. Because of his injured leg, he can't get on his knees, so he sits.

Luigi is whimpering. Franco tells him, "Papa, we need to get you hooked up to the oxygen. Manny, where's the thing?"

"Hold on." Manny unstraps the tank from the wheelchair and moves it so its regulator is near Luigi's head. He pulls the thin plastic tube hand-over-hand. When he's holding the end, where the nostril things are, he hands it to Franco. "Here, Papa," Franco says. He leans forward and fixes the plastic tube on Luigi's head until the oxygen is flowing into his nostrils.

Luigi grabs Franco's arm with his one good hand and pulls him close.

"Take this guy in the warehouse and kill him," he says. "You take care of it yourself."

"I don't want to leave you."

"I'll be okay. Leave Manny with me. I'll wait to hear this guy is dead. Then—after—I'll see a doctor."

"Okay, Papa. Help me up, Manny." Franco holds up his good hand. Manny takes it and pulls him to his feet. "Come on, Roy. Let's go."

Roy grabs the shotgun, and he and Franco walk me out of Luigi's office. We get to the end of the hallway, Franco opens the door and ushers us into the warehouse.

The guy who was with Franco at Maria's house is there. He's talking to another guy. The Yellow Cab is gone.

"Hey, Jerry," Franco says. "Give me a hand."

The guy from Maria's house comes over. "What you need?"

"Grab a bunch of zip ties," Franco tells him. "Okay, Tricky," he says, and he shoves me toward the loading docks. "Keep moving." He and I walk through the loading docks toward the far end of the room, both of us limping. Roy and Jerry are behind us—Roy with the shotgun.

"You been nothing but an aggravation since I met you," Franco says as we walk. "You been lucky, but that's over now."

I don't say anything.

"Where's your pal Joey Romano?" Franco says. "Isn't he

supposed to be protecting you? Doesn't look like he's doing a very good job."

We walk past the last loading dock, we're at the end of the warehouse. Skids of books are lined up against a concrete wall.

"Okay," Franco says. We stop.

"You want the shotgun?" Roy says.

"No, I got a better idea. Let's tie him to one of these skids." He walks along the skids, inspecting them. "Yeah, here we go. Bring him here."

Roy and Jerry walk me to double-stacked skids of Danielle Steel paperbacks.

"Stand him in front of these. Jerry, zip tie his ankles to the bottom pallet."

Jerry gets on his knees and ties my ankles to the wooden pallet under the Steels.

"Okay," he says, getting to his feet.

"Now do his hands."

Jerry lifts my bound hands till they're at the height of the top skid's pallet, about the height of my shoulders. "Hold still," he says. He connects my wrists to the pallet. I'm twisted to one side, my hands together, but otherwise I'm flat against the front of the skids.

"Okay, he can't move, Franco," Jerry says.

Franco walks up close to me. For the first time I notice his eyes are bloodshot. He's not exactly steady on his feet either— something more than the limp. He must still be on drugs from the hospital.

"Dead-Eye Eddy," he says. "Yeah, that's right. I know about your little nickname." He laughs. "My father says you got a spell on me, some gloomy old-world bullshit. But this ain't New Jersey."

I say, "Both times I shot you was accidents, Franco. Ask Jerry. I didn't even know who you were. I helped him put you in the car. Tell him, Jerry."

Jerry shrugs.

Franco goes to the forklift parked nearby. He climbs onto it, turns it on.

He drives the forklift to a skid a few down from the ones I'm tied to, lowers the forks and slips them deep inside its pallet. He lifts the skid a couple feet and backs up, maneuvering until the skid faces me. The back of the forklift faces the dock.

The skid is a newly released hardback—the latest Ludlum.

Franco leans forward and shouts at me, "Okay, Mr. Lucky. Let's see how this works out for you."

Roy gets excited. "You're gonna squish him like a bug!"

I'm thinking I should shut my eyes. Maybe it'll be over quick.

A couple other guys show up, they join Roy and Jerry off to one side.

Franco shifts the forklift into reverse and backs it away from me. "Making room for ramming speed!"

"Yeah!" Roy shouts.

"Go for it, Franco!" another guy says, shaking his fist.

Franco backs up until he's practically against the dock door. He stops, shifts into forward, and, shouting a gleeful and triumphant war cry— "Ya-Hoo!"—he stomps on the accelerator. The forklift, still in reverse, flies backward, smashing into the flimsy metal of the dock door. As the forklift passes through the door, it tips back and falls from view, like it's falling off a cliff, the skid of Ludlums crashing down on top of it.

"Oh no," one of the guys says. He and Roy and Jerry and the fourth guy run to the big, jagged hole in the dock door and look through it, down on the wreckage. If it's a standard height loading dock, the forklift must have fallen four feet, onto concrete.

The four guys run a couple docks down, to a man door that's propped open, and disappear outside.

CHAPTER 48

I CAN'T SEE ANYTHING BUT DAYLIGHT through the hole in the dock door. But I hear the guys outside. They're calling, "Franco? Are you okay? Wake up, Franco! Come on, Franco! Wake up!"

One of them says, "I'm not getting a pulse."

"Oh shit," another one says.

"Poor Franco."

"Let's bring him inside."

A little later, I hear them on metal steps leading up to the man door. Then they come in: the first guy backward, his hands under Franco's arms; Franco, face up and more or less horizontal; then Roy and Jerry, each holding a leg. When they get inside, they stretch Franco out on the concrete floor. They stand around him.

"I can't believe it," one guy says.

"Poor bastard."

"Who's going to tell Luigi?"

"Luigi!" Roy says. "Shit. Luigi."

"I'll tell him," Jerry says. "You guys stay with Franco. And keep an eye on Dead-Eye." He walks to the door leading to Luigi's office. He opens the door and goes through it, letting it shut behind him.

We all wait in silence: me tied to the front of the skids, the three guys standing around Franco. I have no idea what they're thinking about, but I'm thinking about Luigi's temper. I realize, that's probably what's on their minds too.

Jerry comes back through the door. He holds it open, and Luigi comes through in his wheelchair, Manny pushing. Manny brings Luigi to Franco.

"Aye!" Luigi cries. "My Franco! My boy!" He grabs Roy's forearm with his good hand and says, "What happened?"

"He backed the forklift off the dock, Luigi. He never knew what hit him."

"It's my fault!" Luigi says. "I thought he could break the spell this guy had on him. Where is Johnson?"

"There," Roy says, pointing to me.

"Take me to him."

Manny pushes the wheelchair toward me. I squirm around, trying to get free, but it's no use.

When he's stopped in front of me, Luigi says, "You took my Franco."

"I didn't do anything."

"You killed him! My future! My—"

He convulses, jerking up straight in the wheelchair, grabbing at his chest with his good hand. He makes a growling noise, then collapses, falling forward out of the wheelchair onto the concrete floor at my feet.

"What the hell," Manny says. He jerks the chair out of the way and gets on his knees next to Luigi. "Boss!" he says. "Boss!"

He rolls Luigi over. It's obvious he's dead.

Roy and the other guys come running to see what happened.

Manny sits on the floor, nothing he can do.

"He's dead," he tells the others.

"Are you sure?" Jerry says.

"He had a heart attack. He was dead before he hit the floor."

"Jesus," one of the guys says. "Franco and Luigi both."

"What do we do now?" Roy says. "We're screwed."

"I don't get it," Manny says. He's shaking his head. He says, to me, "What's your deal?"

"What do you mean?"

"I put that bomb under your truck myself. I still don't know how you got out of that. There's not a scratch on you. Now this…" He indicates Luigi.

Jerry says, "Seriously, Manny, what do we do? We got no boss. We're in the middle of a war…"

Manny gets up from the floor, brushing his pants. "We make peace with Joey Romano."

"Surrender is more like it," Roy says.

"We just killed D'Adderio. How's he going to let that go?"

"We were just doing our jobs."

"Luigi made us do it."

"We make the peace," Manny says. "This is Joey's city now."

"He's going to need help running it," Jerry says.

"You think he'd hire us?"

"I don't see why not."

"Someone needs to talk to Joey."

"How about him?" Manny says, pointing to me. "Joey knows him. We send him with the news about Luigi and Franco, a message that we want a sit-down."

"What, and just hang around, waiting to see if Joey is going to kill us?" Roy says.

"You got a better idea?"

"I'm with Manny," Jerry says.

Manny says to me, "Would you be willing to do that?"

"Sure," I say, trying to not seem excited.

Manny comes over to me holding a pocketknife. He cuts the zip ties around my wrists.

"Thanks," I say. I rub my wrists while he squats down and cuts the ones around my ankles. He stands again. Putting his knife away, he says, "No hard feelings."

"What about my money?"

"Oh, yeah. Sorry. I forgot."

He digs into a pocket, pulls out the money he took from me during the cab ride over, and hands it to me. I count the hundred-dollar bills. All twenty-five are there. I put them away.

"I'll go see Joey for you guys," I say. "But I need to get something to eat first. And some coffee. I've been up all night. The last time I ate was like lunch yesterday."

"We can get you something to eat," Manny says. "We've got food here."

CHAPTER 49

I WALK WITH Manny, Jerry, and a couple other guys, all the way across the warehouse. To the left of the door that leads to Luigi's office, behind a wall of glass overlooking the loading docks, is a room I didn't notice before. We file into it.

It must be where they take their breaks. It's harshly lit. It has a white linoleum floor, a fridge against one wall, and a long Formica counter with a sink and a coffeemaker and microwave. Two eight-foot tables are in there, each surrounded by cheap folding chairs.

"Have a seat, Eddy," Manny says, pulling out one of the folding chairs. I sit.

"Jerry, get him some coffee."

"What do you take in it, Mr. Johnson?" Jerry says.

"Just black is fine."

"You got it." Jerry goes to the coffeemaker. He looks at the handled glass pot, he says, "Okay, this looks terrible. I'm gonna make a fresh pot."

Manny has the fridge open. He's leaning in, reaching for

something. He pulls out a metal lunch box.

"This is my lunch," he says, putting the box on the table and opening it. "I've got a meatloaf sandwich, how does that sound? My wife makes a killer meatloaf."

"Sounds great."

Manny hands me the sandwich. It's thick and heavy in my hand, wrapped in plastic. I can see there's lots of meat. I unwrap it and take a bite. It's awesome.

"I got some potato chips. You want them?"

I nod yes.

Manny opens a small bag of chips and puts it on the table in front of me.

I take another bite of the sandwich. I look at my watch. It's almost nine o'clock.

The two other guys stand across from me, their butts leaning against the counter. They watch me eat.

Jerry comes back from the coffeemaker. "Fresh coffee on its way," he says.

Still chewing meatloaf, I give him a thumbs up. I grab some potato chips and push them in my mouth.

"Hey, get him a napkin," Manny says. One of the guys turns and grabs a roll of paper towels. He pulls a perforated sheet free, folds it into a triangle, and puts it in front of me. "Paper towels is all we got, Mr. Johnson. Sorry."

"No problem," I say, my mouth half full.

"I'm Frank," the guy says.

"Hey, Frank."

The other guy leaning his butt against the counter says, "What do you think Joey Romano will do, Mr. Johnson?"

"Leave him alone," Manny says. "Let him eat."

"What?" the guy says. "I'm nervous."

"We're all nervous," Jerry says.

"He knows Joey, what does it hurt to ask his opinion?"

"Yeah," Frank says. "What do you think, Mr. Johnson? Should we be worried?"

They're all looking at me.

I swallow what I'm chewing and wipe my mouth with the paper towel. "I think things could work out. Joey's an upbeat guy. He tends to be in a good mood. When he gets the news about Franco and Luigi, my guess is he'll be magnanimous."

"Magnanimous?"

"Not like Luigi," Manny says.

Jerry puts a Styrofoam cup of coffee in front of me. "Here you go, Mr. Johnson. Fresh brewed."

"Thanks." I sip some. It's not bad, a little too hot.

Manny tells Frank, "Go get the cab and pull it around front. I'm gonna use it to drive him to Joey's."

"Okay." Frank leaves.

"I'm ready," I say. I've finished the sandwich, and that was plenty to settle my stomach. "I would like to make a quick phone call, though, before I go." I gesture toward a phone on the wall near the door.

"Sure," Manny says.

I get up and limp to the phone.

"You need to dial one to get outside."

I dial one and there's a dial tone. Then I call Casita Reynoso. Some guy answers.

"I'm calling for Maria Juarez," I say. "Or Elena."

"Hold up," he says. A woman comes on the line. "Hello, this is Elena. How may I help you?"

"This is Eddy Johnson. I have a message for Maria. Tell her there's no more danger." I lower my voice so Manny and the others can't hear me. "The guys who tried to kidnap Raoul are no longer involved. I took care of it."

"Really?"

"Yes. Maria was going to move, but now she doesn't have to. Tell her—it's okay to go back to her house. It's over."

"That's great news," Elena says. "Maria will be very happy."

"Okay. Thanks, Elena."

"Thank *you*, Mr. Eddy."

CHAPTER 50

I'M IN THE BACK SEAT of the Yellow Cab with my cup of coffee. Manny is driving.

We're passing through Apartment City—the sprawling cluster of apartment complexes, convenience stores, and fast-food restaurants along Riverside Drive. There's a couple paperback swap shops in that area, where you can trade two-for-one or get store credit. And in back rooms or after hours you can get a lot more than that.

I say, "I used to live down here when I first moved to Austin."

"You got out. Not everyone does."

"I hated it."

"We call it the hell hole. But it's a place to start. Where'd you move from?"

"Philadelphia."

"Oh yeah? What part?"

"Farther out. More like Camden."

"Talk about a hell hole."

"It was pretty bad."

We get to South Congress, Manny turns right. We head for the bridge.

"So, you don't actually work for Joey, do you?" he says.

"No, I'm on my own. I'm a dealer."

"What kind of stuff?"

"Modern literature—mostly American."

"There's money in that?"

"No. I mean, there can be, but it's not regular."

"I got a piece of this porn shop. That's where the money is."

We cross the river and head up Congress Avenue. Manny takes a right on 2nd Street.

"I'm going to drop you off like a block away," he says.

"Okay."

"We appreciate your helping us out. I'll be at the phone number I gave you in half an hour."

He pulls to the side of the road.

I get out and the cab goes on. I walk toward the Romano Brothers building.

Outside the visitors' entrance, one of Joey's guys is standing around. When he sees me coming, he flicks a cigarette to the curb and perks up.

"Dead-Eye Eddy," he says. "We been wondering where you were. We were afraid the Capalettis got you."

"They did. They sent me with a message for Joey."

"He's in there. Go ahead." He opens the door and I go in.

Carol the deeply tanned receptionist is there. She's behind her desk.

"Heya, Dead-Eye," she says, "Joey's expecting you. He's in his office."

I head down the hallway. When I get to Joey's office, I knock on the door. "Joey, it's Eddy."

"Eddy!" I hear him say. He opens the door.

He doesn't look much better than I do. His hair is messed up and he needs a shave. There's a folding bed in the corner. It's unmade, sheets and blankets bunched up.

"Have a seat, Eddy," he says. I sit in the armchair facing his desk. He goes around and sits in his swivel chair.

"Where have you been? Burnell says he got you out like three hours ago."

"The Capalettis nabbed me. Right outside the police station."

"I knew it. That damn Luigi. So, what—you got away?"

"Sort of. I've got some good news, Joey."

"I can use some."

"Luigi and Franco are dead."

"What do you mean?"

"They're dead, Joey. Both of them."

"Get the hell out of here."

"No, really. Their guys are waiting for you to call so they can hand stuff over to you. They want to work for you now."

"You seen them dead with your own eyes? It sounds like a trap."

"No, they're dead, Joey."

"What happened?"

I tell him.

"Jesus," Joey says.

"I just got lucky is all."

"No, you had Franco's number somehow. It's over my head. He was a tough guy, Eddy."

I shrug. "Anyway, like I said, their guys are ready to talk. Here's the number." I hand Joey the piece of paper. "The main guy, as far as I can tell, is a guy named Manny."

"I'll give him a call," Joey says. "Course it won't hurt to make them wait a little. In the meantime, let's celebrate."

"I'd like to celebrate with a shower and a change of clothes."

Joey laughs. "I hear you," he says.

He swings his chair around, grabs two empty glasses and a round tin with a bottle of single malt scotch inside. "This'll have to do for now." He pulls the bottle from the tin. "Some guy gave me this. I can't pronounce it, but it's the smoothest damn thing I ever drank." He pours some into both glasses and hands me one.

"Salute, Eddy," he says, lifting his glass. I lift mine too, we clink and drink. The scotch is delicious.

"I been dreaming of this, Eddy. I been biding my time. I figured it wouldn't be long before Luigi would croak, and then I could make a move on Franco. But you… You come along and, bing bang, you start a war. I hardly know what's going on, you've already wiped them out… Now I'm in control of the city. I've got Miller in my pocket."

"Well, not exactly. We haven't talked yet about what happened at the Fiscal."

"Poor Sonny. But, you know, in his family, being shot by cops is like dying of natural causes."

"But Joey, listen. Before Sonny got killed—when we gave the photographs to Miller—one of them was missing. Miller kind of freaked out. We told him it wasn't your fault, but he was so upset, he didn't know what to think."

"Someone held one back?"

"It's okay, I got it. I figured out who had it and bought it from them."

Joey laughs. "More single malt for Eddy," he says. He reaches across the desk and gives me a generous pour. "You keep surprising me."

"I'm just trying to stay ahead of trouble."

"You've got it with you?"

I nod.

"Let me see." I get the Polaroid from my pocket and hand it to him.

He looks at it a while. Shaking his head, he says, "This Miller guy is really something."

"He's pretty wild."

Joey drops the photo on his desk.

"All right. Excellent. So, you'll take this to him, everything is copacetic."

"Okay but… If I do that, Joey, am I off the hook? Does that make us even?"

"We're way past even, Eddy. I'm in *your* debt."

"No, Joey."

"Seriously. You need to come work for me. I'll make you rich."

"I'm a loner, Joey. You know that. I'm glad we got everything straightened out. But when the dust settles, I just want my old life back."

"You sure?"

"I appreciate the offer."

"Well, then let me ask you something. What does that look like? What would it take? To get you back to normal?"

"I don't know…"

"No, really. I could be like one of those nature guys that helps push a whale back into the ocean."

"Well, I need a car. The Capalettis blew up my truck."

"Done. What else?"

"The other thing is, it looks like I'm gonna get kicked out of the Alamo. Once Miller gets elected, he's going to tear it down to make way for this big development he has planned."

"And you like it there? You could do a lot better, Eddy."

"I don't know… I like being downtown…"

"Okay, I'll tell you what. I'm gonna hold onto this photo. I'll deal with Miller. I'll see what I can do. Maybe he *doesn't* tear it down."

"Really? That'd be awesome, Joey."

"I'll give it a shot. What else?"

"That's it."

Joey pushes a button on his desk phone and Carol says, "Yeah? What?"

"Tell Tony to bring the Lincoln around."

"Gotcha," Carol says. Joey pushes the button again. He says to me, "Okay, here's what's going to happen. Tony's gonna drive you to a car lot I work with up on North Lamar. I'll tell the guy you're coming. You pick out whatever car you want, it's yours. I'm gonna call this Manny guy. I figure he's probably waited long enough by now."

He stands and comes around his desk. I get up.

"Now listen," he says. "Come around once in a while." He grabs my left shoulder and gives it a squeeze.

"I will, Joey."

"You need anything, you let me know."

CHAPTER 51

I'M IN THE BACK SEAT of the blue Lincoln. Tony's driving me up North Lamar. Other than saying hello when I got in the car, he hasn't talked. He's tense, watching other cars, glancing in his rear-view mirror. He doesn't know the war with the Capalettis is over. It's not my place to tell him and, anyway, I don't feel like talking. I'm wiped out. He'll get the good news soon enough.

He pulls into the middle turn lane to make a left and turns into a used car lot. Behind rows of dusty cars with fluorescent prices on their windshields, there's a billboard-size sign that says *Payday Motors* and *Don't Walk! See Hawk!* Under the sign there's a beat-up old trailer that must be the office.

It's not a reputable place. The vehicles are all under two grand and it's hard to imagine any are bargains. As if he can read my mind, Tony says, "Don't worry, this guy will take good care of you. The last thing he wants is to make Joey mad."

"Thanks, Tony," I say. "And thanks for the ride." I get out of the Lincoln, Tony backs up and leaves, heading south.

A slight breeze is fluttering strings of colorful pennants that crisscross the lot overhead.

A tall slender man wearing snakeskin boots and a black cow-boy hat comes out of the trailer.

"Well now, pardner," he says. "What can I do you for?"

"I need something to drive."

"Anything catch your eye? Any of these beauties would be a good choice." He waves an arm to indicate the sketchy cars all around us. "What kind of a budget are we on? And keep in mind: ten percent down gets you behind the wheel. You can use our weekly payment plan."

"Joey Romano sent me," I say.

"Oh. You're Mr. Romano's associate. My mistake, friend. I've got *your* car behind the trailer. You don't want any of these beaters."

I walk with him behind the trailer. In back, next to a tow truck, is a big red Cadillac. It's gorgeous, with a white leather interior. It can't be more than a couple years old.

"This is *your* car," he says. "I been driving it for a couple months now and I can tell you, she's smooth as silk. I need to get my golf clubs and a couple other things out of the trunk and she's all yours. She's even got a full tank of gas."

"I can't drive around in a car like this," I say.

"Too big? You want something sporty? I got a nice little BMW you can have. It's not here right now."

"No," I say. "I can't have a fancy car. I'm a book dealer. If I drive a car like this, everyone's going to think I have money. I need to look like I can't make ends meet."

"I hear you. But you understand, I have to make sure Mr. Romano is happy. What's he going to think if I send you away in a junker?"

I say, "If you can put me in a pickup truck maybe ten years old, that's reliable, with good tires, I'll make sure Joey knows I'm happy."

SIX MONTHS LATER

I'M IN MY ROOM, sitting in the chair by the window, sipping some bourbon before dinner. Below in the street I can see my truck where it's parked. Behind it is a wooden construction barrier surrounding a pit big enough and deep enough that you could bury a million V. C. Andrews paperbacks in it. On the barrier, a sign says: *Santa Anna Residential Towers—Coming Soon!*

The construction project surrounds the Alamo but, sure enough, thanks to Joey, the Alamo has been spared. Next to its front entrance it now sports a brass plaque identifying it as a historical landmark.

When I finish the glass of bourbon, I put on a jacket and leave my room. I go downstairs to the lobby. It's deserted.

Outside, I get in my truck and drive the few minutes it takes me to get to Casita Reynoso. It's only six-thirty, but already there's a line coming out the door, which is propped open so the clusters of well-dressed people standing around on the sidewalk can hear when the hostess calls their names.

I drive around the block, up the alley, and park behind the

restaurant. I go in the back door. The kitchen is a whirlwind of activity—half a dozen cooks in whites rushing this way and that, calling to each other. Now and then a broiler flares up.

Vincent, the head cook, comes by hugging a plastic tub full of chickens. "Hola, Eddy," he says. "The usual?"

"Yes, Vincent. Thanks." I go to the wooden table in the corner and sit.

Maria comes in from the dining room, still writing some details on a ticket before giving it to one of the cooks. She sees me at the table and smiles.

"Eddy," she says. "I didn't know if you would be here tonight." She brings me a plastic glass of water and a silverware set. "I'm glad you came."

I'm smiling.

"Listen," she says, looking for something in her apron pocket. "I'm having a party for Raoul this Saturday. It's his birthday." She pulls a little flyer out and puts it on the table. It's colorful, with a picture of a birthday cake and a piñata. "It starts at noon."

"Okay, sure. I'll come by," I say. "Thanks."

"I'm making a tres leches cake."

One of the cooks comes over. "Here you go, Mr. Eddy." He slides a platter onto the table in front of me: my usual. Black beans just a little soupy, with some grilled chorizo chopped in, two eggs over easy on top. Oh man! Maria pulls a salt shaker from her apron pocket and hands it to me.

"Order up!" Vincent calls from the pickup station behind her. "Maria!"

She turns and loads plated meals onto a big oval tray. She lifts the tray up high, balancing it with one hand centered under it, and backs her way through the swinging door to the dining room, knocking the door open first with a swish of her hips.

☰　　☰　　☰

Before heading back to my room, I decide to drop by the Dusty Jacket. That's kind of become my go-to spot since the night my truck blew up. I park out front and go in.

The place is more lively than usual. I feel lucky to find a place at the bar, and quickly go sit there. "Bunch of librarians in town for a convention," Jack says, putting a Shiner Bock in front of me. *Librarians*, I think. *Cheerfully defacing books for centuries.*

One of them, a pale young man, is sitting on the bar stool to my right, drinking what looks like a piña colada.

"Hello," he says. "Dan Bradley. I'm from Ohio."

"You with the librarians thing?" I say.

"Yep. I'm with the Kent State Library. Pleased to meet you."

"I'm Eddy," I say. "Eddy Johnson. I'm a book dealer."

"Oh. A dealer." I can see he's put off a little.

Jack swings by and pours me a shot of Johnnie Walker. He says to Dan Bradley from Ohio, "You got any idea who this is you're talking to?"

Dan Bradley is confused. He looks at me, his head tilted a little.

Jack says, "This is Dead-Eye Eddy, the guy who saved the Alamo."

ACKNOWLEDGMENTS

THANKS TO Page Wiley and Leonard Volk who urged me to finish this. To my former colleagues at Half Price Books. To Amber Kuehner at Granville Milling, who is still selling the heck out of my first novel, *An Inconvenient Herd*. To Emily Hitchcock and her team at Columbus Publishing Lab, highly recommended. In memory of Pierre Francois Gregory, Kent Hedtke, Ruth and Kelly Raines.

ABOUT THE AUTHOR

JOHN WILEY SPENDS most of his time writing and farming.

He and his wife Marie live in central Ohio, on a one-hundred-acre farm that is somewhat isolated but happens to be at the center of the universe. They have, in addition to cattle, Ridgebacks and Tennessee Walkers and indoor/outdoor cats, snapping turtles in the pond, turkey buzzards circling overhead, groundhogs tunneling, coyotes calling to each other in the night.

Eddy Johnson, Book Dealer features Austin, Texas, as it was when John and Marie lived there in the 1980s. They worked in bookstores then (Half Price Books!) and met a variety of colorful book dealers, reprobates all.

John likes hearing from readers, and he invites you to contact him directly at upthelane@hotmail.com.

More From
John Wiley

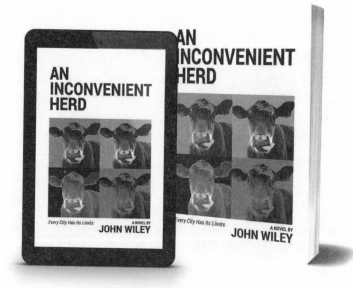

**Available now as a paperback and
e-book at all online retailers, or ask for
it at your favorite local bookstore.**

In Praise of *An Inconvenient Herd*

A fun, goofy book...I laughed out loud many times... What a charming book... This book made me ridiculously happy. I truly adore it... Just thinking about this book makes me smile...Delightful!...Hilarious... This book will lift you up... Worth reading more than once... Witty political sattire...

—A bouquet of positive comments from
Goodreads and Amazon.com reviews

SOMEONE LETS FARMER'S COWS OUT. Fueled by idealism and curiosity, the herd follows a bike path into the big city, chasing a dream of a new way of life. The good-natured cattle make lots of friends, but life in town is complicated. They encounter religion, local politics, and manicured lawns. Meanwhile, Farmer is frantically searching for the the wayward cows, racing to save them from the perils of celebrity and the urban machine before its too late.